Lucky in Love

Amelia Judd

Cover design by LLewellen Designs
Edited by Karen Dale Harris
Proofread by Daisycakes Creative Services

Published by Mitchell Davis Press, LLC

www.ameliajudd.com

ISBN-10: 1-946517-08-9
ISBN-13: 978-1-946517-08-1

To all the soccer moms I've shared the sidelines with
You're my fierce, loyal, and loving teammates ...
Lucky in Love is for you!

ONE

CLAIRE Bennett glanced at the high-tech watch strapped to her wrist and repressed a groan. Touted as the best smart watch on the market, the darn thing cost a fortune and promised to manage her hectic schedule with ease. But she was a single mom with a full-time career. Not even the sharpest of cutting-edge technology could totally subdue her schedule.

The tension flowing through her solidified into a tight knot between her shoulder blades. She prided herself on efficiency and hated running late—especially tonight. Talk about amping up the strain of an already crappy situation.

Forcing a smile, Claire reminded herself to consider tonight nothing more than a business meeting. She hurried into the small bar a few miles outside of the lakeside town of Silver Bay, Wisconsin and scanned the room for single men. Or to be precise, one single man—one, *lucky*, single man.

Three booths in, she spotted a middle-aged guy with brown hair, faded jean shorts, a Packer's muscle shirt, and a saggy tattoo of a … She tipped her head and squinted for a closer inspection. Recognition dropped her stomach. A cheesehead. The man had permanently imprinted a giant cheesehead on his bicep.

Brown hair, Packer's shirt, and left-arm tattoo—those were the three identifiers her good friend Deb Saunders had given her. This guy must be Lucky.

Oh, lucky her.

Claire blew out a breath long enough to inflate her kids' favorite pool toy. She should have refused to meet Deb's cousin as soon as she heard his ridiculous name. But after a month-long covert—and totally unproductive—search for a fake boyfriend on her own, Claire needed help. Of course, she'd sworn Deb to secrecy before asking for assistance. A fake boyfriend that everyone knew was fake would be as useful as an uncharged smartphone.

After hearing her dilemma, Deb had immediately suggested her cousin Lucky, whom she called mature. While a desirable trait for a fake boyfriend, Claire had been thinking Lucky would be a George Clooney mature rather than a Larry the Cable Guy mature.

"Hey, honey," her prospective fake boyfriend yelled to a passing waitress, "I need another refill." He shook a glass full of ice at the young girl. "And keep 'em coming, doll. I'll be here for hours."

The last of Claire's mustered smile drained away as she watched Lucky the Cable Guy pour ice into his mouth and start chomping. His bulging belly bounced against the edge of the table. Little shards of ice flew from his open mouth with each enthusiastic crunch.

She glanced over her shoulder at the door and contemplated slinking out of the bar before he noticed her. But the thought of her impending public humiliation did a grand job of raising her blood pressure, planting her feet, and steeling her resolve. She had a bachelorette auction to get out of, damn it. Like it or not, Lucky the Cable Guy looked to be her best way out.

Claire tried to be optimistic. Maybe he was really nice. Sure, his attire suggested demolition derby rather than blind date—or business date to be more accurate—but Deb had assured her of his sweetness.

Time to woman-up.

She strode toward Lucky's table. A step away from him—and from a night of likely talking about the Pack while suppressing cringes and dodging flying ice chips—she felt the air shift and a flutter warm her skin.

On instinct, she turned her head and locked eyes with a good-looking guy staring at her from a few tables away. He seemed vaguely familiar, but she couldn't imagine meeting someone that attractive and not remembering him. A snug-fitting Green Bay pullover covered wide shoulders and well-defined arms. Thick, tousled dark-brown hair framed a face any men's fitness magazine would be proud to display.

But no tattoo. Or at least, she couldn't tell if he had one since the pullover covered his left bicep.

Head cocked to the side, he studied her with a curious expression and a slight, mischievous upturn of his full lips. His brilliant blue eyes were full of both good-natured humor and—okay, she might be imagining it—a sensual, spellbinding scrutiny that said he could see straight to her soul and liked everything he saw.

Whoa. Where had that come from? She clenched her jaw and drew in a breath. She was here to negotiate a business deal. Nothing more.

And the first order of business was figuring out which Lucky might be her intended date for the evening: Lucky the Cable Guy or Lucky the Male Paragon?

They both had brown hair, and each was wearing a Packers shirt. One Lucky had a visible tattoo on his bicep. Long sleeves covered the other Lucky's arms, making it impossible to tell if he had a tattoo or not.

Why hadn't she asked Deb for a more definite way to ID the guy? But, come on, who would've thought somebody named Lucky would be that difficult to spot? Lesson learned. Next time Claire arranged a meeting to proposition a stranger in a bar, she'd establish a more thorough identification system well in advance.

"Hindsight," she muttered to herself, eyeing her two options.

Lucky the Cable Guy shook more ice into his mouth and started scratching his rounded belly when he noticed her looking at him. "Hey, doll," he said, holding eye contact for approximately one second before he locked in on her chest. "Name's Earl." He licked his lips. "Have a seat, and I'll buy ya a drink."

Earl, not Lucky. Claire leaned down until her eyes were again in his line of sight. "I can't tell if you meant that offer for me or my breasts."

He snorted a laugh. "Both of ya are welcome to join me."

"Sorry, Earl, I can't tonight." She straightened to her full height and muttered, "I've got a problem to solve."

Lucky the Male Paragon quirked an eyebrow at her, and a grin tugged at the corners of his lips. A disorienting jolt of female awareness shot through her. Could this gorgeous guy actually be Deb's cousin?

Claire squared her shoulders. Only one way to find out. Holding his gaze, she moved forward. Known for being cool under pressure, she oversaw multimillion-dollar deals on a daily basis. She could negotiate one small personal transaction.

He rose to his feet. And then he smiled … and the earth tilted on its axis, bowing to the perfection of his dimple-framed, high-wattage, hypnotic smile.

Holy smokes. Her step faltered, and she actually felt short of breath. *Get a grip*, she silently ordered. Then resisting an eye roll, she sucked in air to help focus her oxygen-deprived brain.

She stopped directly in front of him and tipped her head back to maintain eye contact. He must be about six inches taller than her, which would put him a little over six feet. He looked younger than she'd expected from Deb's description, but so what if he looked young? She'd always looked young for her age as well.

She cleared her throat and smiled wide. "Are you … Lucky?"

•••

Ethan DuBois flashed another smile at the classy blonde in the sleek blue dress. As a recently retired professional soccer player, he'd been hit on by countless women in countless ways. He thought he'd heard all the lines before, but this one was new. He always appreciated originality.

"Absolutely," he answered, more than happy to

play along. He'd noticed her the moment she stepped through the door. Her wide, expressive eyes and sweet smile said girl-next-door. Her lean curves and long legs were more femme-fatale. The intriguing mix was enough to make any guy take notice.

"I'm Claire." She inclined her head toward his table. "Can I join you for a drink while we talk?"

Her words were forward—her demeanor, tentative. The contradiction turned intriguing into intoxicating.

He grinned and gestured to the empty seat across from his. As soon as they sat down, the waitress returned to the table to take their drink order. Claire gave the girl her full attention as she placed her order. Extending the simple gesture of respect went a long way in Ethan's book.

When the waitress left to get his unexpected date an iced tea and another beer for him, Claire turned to study him with the most vibrant eyes he'd ever seen. They were blue and green and golden and intently locked on him.

He'd had his share of women eyeball him, but she wasn't stripping him down or trying to appear sultry and seductive. Instead, her appraisal suggested she was searching deeper, beyond the exterior many recognized but few tried to look beneath.

"I hear you're new in town."

"Arrived a few days ago." Ethan wondered what else she'd heard about him.

"Huh." She tilted her head to the side, her thick blond hair sliding temptingly over one shoulder. "I thought you'd been here a couple of months. No matter." She gave her head a quick shake. "Hope you don't mind if I cut to the chase and discuss the terms of my proposition."

Ethan blinked. He opened his mouth but had no frigging clue what to say. Thankfully, the waitress returned with their drinks, giving him a moment to wrap his head around Claire's bombshell.

Becoming a professional soccer player at eighteen had forced him to grow up quickly. He'd been surrounded by guys older—and usually wiser—than him about soccer and about life. He'd watched, listened, learned. And now, at the age of twenty-nine, he felt much older than his years—especially with his body reminding him daily of the wear and tear he'd put it through playing the sport he loved.

He couldn't remember the last time he'd felt this frigging naive. *Proposition?* Damn, how had he read her so wrong? He'd never paid for sex in his life and sure as hell wasn't starting now.

But for some reason, he sat back in the booth, waiting. The server left, and Claire glanced around the room as if making sure no undercover cops were close enough to hear what was likely to be her very interesting—if illegal—proposition. He cocked an eyebrow at her, expecting her to name her price.

Instead, her brow crinkled, and she ran her tongue across her lower lip.

He stared at the full, soft flesh. Heat warmed his blood. She was smooth; he'd give her that. He'd better be careful or he'd be reconsidering his moral stance against paying for sex.

"I need a boyfriend until mid-October," she blurted. "I'm willing to pay you two thousand dollars to play the part." She paused, toying with the heart-shaped silver pendant around her neck. "But you can't tell anyone we aren't actually dating. And, of course, you won't be able to date anyone else during our relationship. I need for us to look exclusive."

If Ethan had been surprised before, he was dumbstruck now.

Claire wasn't selling.

She was buying.

Doing his damnedest to hide his surprise, he leaned forward, propped his elbows on the table, and steepled his hands. He had to admit, her desire to purchase his services intrigued him. He narrowed his eyes as if considering her offer—which, hell, he kinda was—and tried to decide which of his many questions to ask first.

He started with the obvious. "What *services* would be required of me?"

"Nothing distasteful. I only require a pretend boyfriend, not a real one." Claire's words were now crisp and professional. The blush crawling up her neck, not so much.

"Not sure you could suggest anything I'd find distasteful."

The blush spread to her cheeks. "We'd need to go on dates to be seen in public. And"—she grimaced—"you'll have to meet my sister Kat."

"Judging by the way you said that, I'm guessing she'll be a tough sell."

"My youngest sister is the reason for this charade."

"Let me guess. She stole your boyfriend, and now you want to bring a smoking hot date to their wedding?" he asked with a wink.

Claire shook her head. "Wrong on both counts. Kat's already married, and I don't have a problem attending weddings alone."

"Why then?"

"Let's just say that when Kat sets her sights on an objective, she goes about achieving it with hurricane-force tenacity." Claire sounded both frustrated and amused. "I've found it's often wiser to bunker down than confront her head-on."

He grinned. "So I'm a storm shelter."

"Of sorts. What do you say, Lucky? Are you interested?"

"Why not?" He shrugged. He'd always made decisions quickly. Trusting his gut had saved his ass in more soccer matches than he could count. And right now, his gut said that pretending to date the beautiful Claire for the next few months would be an entertaining distraction from the real reason he'd come back to town—dealing with his mother's stubbornness.

"Excellent." She nodded in confirmation. "Let's start by going to dinner two weeks from Friday at Bayside. It's downtown on the main square, so plenty of people will see us together."

"If you really want to get the rumors started, I could sleep over after dinner." He gave her his best look of innocence.

"Sheesh." She rolled her eyes but couldn't hide the flicker of humor in their depths. "Cool your jets, Lucky. We're only talking a few fake dates. Neither of us will actually be getting lucky in the next two months."

"If we're supposedly dating that long, people are going to assume we're getting busy."

"Exactly," she said with satisfaction. "Assumptions will get the job done. That way there's no reason for us to actually 'get busy,' as you say."

"I can think of a few good ones."

Her lips twitched, and for an instant, he thought she might actually laugh.

Then she schooled her features into a businesslike expression. "If I pay you less, will you take it down a notch or two?"

"I'll let you in on a secret … " He leaned forward, motioning with his index finger for her to come a little closer, his most charming smile firmly in place.

Laughter played around her lips. She tilted her head and shifted her eyes to the side, letting out a sexy little sigh—obviously trying to decide whether or not to play along. "Fine," she eventually conceded. She folded her hands on the table and leaned forward until her face was distractingly close. She raised one eyebrow in silent challenge.

Damn, she smelled good—almost tropical and completely feminine. He swallowed a groan when she licked her lips in what seemed a nervous tell. Her tongue slid across the soft, slick flesh, sending his pulse into overdrive.

He'd kicked off the game, but the arousal stirring through him made it clear she'd now gained offensive possession.

"What's your secret, Lucky?"

The breathy whisper brushed across his skin and sent a fresh wave of desire heading south. Trying to cool off before his interest became too obvious, Ethan drew in another lungful of air. Which completely backfired. With her so near, all he could smell was the delicious coconut and pineapple scent rising from her glossy, golden hair.

"Well, Claire"—he held her gaze in his heated one—"I only know how to provide top-notch service. So, you're going to get the same completely focused, extremely thorough, and totally dedicated level of performance no matter what you pay me." He kept his voice low and intimate. "And just out of curiosity … Why do you keep calling me Lucky?"

Her eyes widened and her brows arched into a what-the-hell-are-you-talking-about expression. "You said your name was Lucky."

"Actually, you asked if I *was* lucky." He flashed her a cocky grin. "And tonight, when you walked up to my table, I was feeling pretty lucky."

TWO

CLAIRE shot from the booth in a rush of motion. Mouth agape, she stared down at the stranger she'd just propositioned and shook her head in denial. "I was supposed to meet Deb's cousin Lucky here at seven o'clock. Is that you?"

"Afraid not." He gave a careless one-shoulder shrug. "I don't have any cousins. Always wanted a few if that helps."

"No," she hissed. "That doesn't help." A little ticked and a lot embarrassed, she scrunched her eyes closed and tipped her head back so she didn't have to look at his handsome face. Honest to God, she couldn't figure out if she felt lucky or unlucky to find out he wasn't Lucky.

"Unless you want everyone in the place to notice," he said, "you might want to sit back down."

Claire snapped her eyes open. Her abrupt flight from the table had drawn the attention of multiple patrons in the little bar. They were watching her with an unveiled curiosity that signaled she was in danger of engaging Silver Bay's rumor mill.

She took a fortifying breath and slid back into the booth. "Thought I saw a mouse," she announced to no-one in particular. She turned back to Lucky, narrowing her eyes. "Turns out it was a rat."

Chuckling, he lifted his hands in a palms-out, don't-shoot gesture. "I didn't know you were looking for another guy, I swear. But does it really matter which one of us helps you out?"

Claire grabbed her phone from her purse. "I don't even know you," she answered, tapping a frantic message to Deb. She hit send and looked up at him. "You could be a felon. Or worse ... " She gasped, studying his face more closely. "Are you younger than me?"

"Hmm." He arched his brow and dipped his head slightly forward and to the right, humor dancing in his eyes. "I'm not sure that's worse."

"Oh my God. How old are you?" She rubbed her fingertips in frantic circles against the tension building behind her temples. "Wait!" She shot out her hand. "Don't tell me. I don't want to know."

"Twenty-nine," he said with a boyish smile, showcasing those dimples.

"I said I didn't want to know!"

"Why not?"

"Because I'm four years older than you." She propped her elbows on the table and covered her eyes. "I'm a cougar," she mumbled, horrified.

"I'm almost thirty if it helps."

"It doesn't." She shook her head. "Deal's off. I need to find an older pretend boyfriend."

"You're firing me because I'm younger than you? Isn't that age discrimination? Even if we overlook the legality of that move, do you really want to go through this interview process again with another guy?"

Damn him for being right. At least about the last

part. If she turned down his offer to help, she'd be back to square one with no idea how to get to square two. She perked up when her watch buzzed with an incoming text. Maybe Deb had tracked down the real Lucky.

Claire glanced at the message. Loaded with cringing emojis and apologies, Deb's text explained the real Lucky had been taken off the market by a biker chick named Roberta he'd met at the Beers 'n Brats Fest the night before.

Resisting a sigh, Claire mentally crossed another option from her dwindling list and contemplated the best course of action. She could get auctioned off on stage in the middle of town while everyone— including her happily remarried ex-husband— assumed she needed charity to get one flipping date. She could try to find an older guy willing to fake a relationship with her until after the auction. Or she could take this Lucky up on his offer to help.

"Here's the thing, Lucky."

"Name's Ethan," he said in a smooth voice.

"Sheesh, even your name sounds young." She blew out a breath. "Here's the thing, *Ethan*. I have two amazing kiddos. I can't let them get hurt in all of this nonsense. If we do this, I'm okay with them thinking I'm casually dating someone, but that's it. With my sister, however, we would need to present our relationship as exclusive."

"Why fake a relationship for her benefit?" He leaned back and eyed her with interest.

She took a sip of tea, stalling until she decided how much information to share.

"Come on, Claire. Silver Bay's the size of a soccer pitch. I'm going to hear about whatever is going on between you two."

"She tricked me into volunteering for a bachelorette auction," Claire admitted through clenched teeth. "If I'm dating someone, I can get out of it."

She chose to leave out the part about how Kat had used Claire's staid reputation to persuade other reluctant singles to participate in the charity event. If a no-nonsense businesswoman like Claire was taking part in the fun, so should they. If Claire wasn't so ticked at her sister for attempting to force her into dating, she'd be happy something good had finally come from her irksome all-work-and-no-play reputation.

"Why can't you tell her no?" Ethan asked. "Don't get me wrong. I'm happy to help, and my schedule is open right now." He shrugged. "Just seems like you're going to a lot of trouble when you could just say no."

"It's not easy to tell Kat no."

Plus, she was sick and tired of the entire town treating her like some fragile bird with a broken wing since getting divorced nearly four years ago. If the near constant attempts to set her up on a date with somebody's brother, son, cousin, neighbor, or husband's friend's co-worker from a previous job—true story—were anything to go by, then the well-meaning residents of Silver Bay thought being in a relationship was her only chance at "healing."

But the divorce hadn't broken her; it had made her realize a few important things about herself and about relationships. Not only had she learned better than to trust the blinding bliss of romance, she'd learned that she might not be the type of person who could share her life with someone else.

If she did ever decide to take a chance on another relationship, it would be on her terms, not because her sister, or mom, or even her own kiddos were bugging her to find someone new. No, she didn't need to be healed. She just needed people to stop meddling in her love life.

"Trust me," she said, turning her focus back to Ethan. "My best bet is hiring a pretend boyfriend so that I have a legitimate reason to gracefully withdraw my name."

He cocked a judgmental eyebrow.

"Okay, fine," she snapped. "I blew past legitimate and graceful the minute I propositioned you." She waved her hand in a dismissive gesture. "But I can still get out of this with some help, and I'm willing to pay big money for that help."

"Does that mean I'm hired again?" Ethan asked.

Judging by his hopeful expression, Claire figured he must really need the cash. Come to think of it, he did mention having an open schedule. "This is only part-time work, you realize," she said, unease crawling up her spine. "I don't want to interfere with your day job."

"I'm retired," he responded in a chipper tone. "But I'm starting a part-time volunteer position next week."

Claire somehow managed to resist clunking her head onto the scarred wooden table between them. Retired translated to jobless. What would people say when they found out the guy she was seeing was years younger than her and unemployed?

She took a few deep breaths while the term "sugar mama" reverberated through her head. Okay, she should cut him some slack. He'd just moved to Silver Bay. He'd probably get a job soon. As long as he didn't live in his mother's basement, all would be okay.

"Any chance you live in your mom's basement?"

"Heck no." He chuckled. "Her guest room is much nicer. Plus, it has an attached bathroom," he said with no hint of apology or embarrassment on his handsome, wrinkle-free face.

Claire's mouth dropped open and a pained sound—some sort of bizarre mixture of a groan and whine—escaped from the back of her throat. This guy needed some serious direction in his life.

"Ethan, you gotta get your act together. You're almost thirty. Don't you want a place of your own? And a job?"

"Don't worry about me." He winked, mischief dancing in the depths of his bright-blue eyes. "I have a little saved up from my last gig."

Too afraid to ask about his last "gig," Claire let that comment go. Ethan was likely one of those guys who got through life on charm and good looks rather than hard work, dedication, and drive. He was the opposite of mature. Maybe spending time with a responsible adult like her would be good for him.

And maybe—Claire brightened as an idea bubbled to life—letting her sister and the good residents of Silver Bay believe she'd picked up a young, carefree stud would finally convince people she wasn't so boring after all. In a moment of blinding, blissful clarity, she realized Ethan's age and lack of planning for the future were the best features she could ask for in a pretend boyfriend. Not only would she get out of the bachelorette auction, she would show everyone that she didn't need to be set up on a blind date with their dog-sitter's stepbrother to add excitement to her life. After all, what could be more exciting than dating a younger-than-her, devil-may-care hottie who could never be considered marriage material for a responsible single mom?

"You're hired," Claire announced, her excitement elevating her volume a few levels. She glanced around to confirm no one had overheard before slipping a business card from her purse. "My mobile number is listed here." She slid the card across the table and tapped the glossy top with her manicured nail. "Please text me your number when you have a moment."

"Sure thing, Boss." The moment he looked at the card, his expression morphed from playful to surprised. "You're Claire Bennett from Bennett Industries, the big cabinet manufacturer?"

"Is that a problem?"

"So Richard Bennett is ... ?" he prompted.

"My father."

"And how old are your kids?"

"Grace turned nine a few days ago. Ty turned ten last month. Why?"

Ethan nodded his head and stared at her with interest for a long beat. "Just curious," he said. "So, what's the next step for our blossoming pretend relationship?"

"The auction is in mid-October. We have between now and then to convince my sister we're in an exclusive relationship. That gives us nine weeks. Let's start with the date at Bayside I mentioned. Two weeks from Friday. That will give me time to lay the groundwork with my family. Then we can go out once a week until the auction." She ran the numbers in her head. "That should be enough dates to convince Kat we're exclusive."

Ethan studied her with an unreadable expression. "You've given this a lot of thought."

"It's what I do."

He blinked. "This"— he motioned between them with his index finger—"is what you do?"

"Well, no. Not *this* exactly," Claire conceded. "But I do enjoy strategizing and implementing business plans. Which brings me to the next detail. As far as paying for our dates, I'd like to take turns so it appears we're both equally vested in the relationship. You can, of course, submit an expense report at the end. I'll reimburse you." She paused, recalling his current lack of employment, and added as gently as possible, "Or do you need me to provide you with a cash advance for expenses?"

"Nah." He gave another carefree one-shoulder shrug. "I can scrape some change together."

Claire almost grinned at the image of Ethan paying for a date with a handful of quarters and crumbled up dollar bills. She couldn't wait for Kat to catch wind of her new boyfriend. She'd never be able to accuse Claire of being boring or lacking spontaneity again.

She rose from the table. "I look forward to doing business with you." She extended her right hand to Ethan, more from habit than thought.

He stood and stepped closer. "Me too," he murmured, a seductive tone edging his voice.

As his fingers closed around hers, her pulse thudded and she felt her eyes go glassy. A moment later, Claire sucked in a quick breath and snatched her hand back.

Turning from Ethan, she made a quick mental note to keep contact with him to a minimum.

As she walked from the bar, all in all, she felt pretty darn good about her progress. She simply needed to keep her physical attraction to him in check. But she wasn't worried about crossing that line. She knew better than to get swept away in physical attraction and the swirling, disorienting—and ultimately fading—fog of romance.

Claire had made that mistake once and wouldn't make it again.

THREE

"I can't think of a better way to spend a lovely August day than having lunch with my three beautiful daughters." Ann Bennett beamed a serene smile at Claire, Hannah, and Kat. "It means the world to me that you take time from your busy schedules to spend with me and with each other."

Claire was the one who'd invited everyone to lunch. Successful plans were built on well-laid foundations after all.

They were seated around an outdoor table on the oversized balcony of the Grand Adelaide Resort, a luxury hotel and spa located outside of Silver Bay. The Victorian-themed Adelaide sat on a sprawling piece of lakefront property. It boasted a beautiful atrium, a top-rate golf course, elegant hotel rooms, and spacious villas.

Families came for the beach in the summer and the indoor waterpark in the winter. While companies from all over the Midwest, including Bennett Industries, held annual meetings in its modern conference center, couples traveled from around the country to enjoy the resort's romantic atmosphere and renowned wedding planner.

On a rainy summer day eleven years ago, she'd

married Jack—the supposed love of her life—in the resort's stately ballroom. Today, she'd arranged lunch with her mom and sisters to subtly drop a mention of her upcoming date with a new man into their conversation.

As promised, Ethan had texted her yesterday with his mobile number and told her he looked forward to their first date in two weeks. He'd even signed the text with the four-leaf clover emoji, cheerfully embracing his new nickname.

"I'm glad everyone was available," Claire said. "I thought it would be nice to share a meal without my kiddos asking 'can we go yet' every five minutes." She suppressed any guilt at the white lie.

"Bennett's currently strapped into a baby carrier on Logan's chest," Kat said, sliding dramatic sunglasses onto her petite nose while the wind tossed her long, dark hair into a wild, graceful disarray that fit her personality perfectly. "He should be good through nap time."

Hannah—whose brown hair was efficiently pulled into a low pony and thus impervious to the lakefront gusts—eyed Kat in confusion. "Isn't Logan at the gym? Before I left work, my last customer grabbed a smoothie and mentioned he was headed there next."

Kat's husband, Logan, owned a very successful training facility in downtown Silver Bay, not far from Hannah's coffee shop, Fresh.

Kat waved away the question with a delicate flick of her wrist. "Logan can make his clients sweat through their customized routines with or without a four-month-old attached to his chest. Plus, he loves showing off Bennett at the gym." She chuckled.

"He's crazy proud of that kid."

"He's a darling baby," Ann said, practically radiating joy. "You two are doing a wonderful job raising him."

Kat shot her sisters a smug smile. "Did you hear that? My awesome parenting skills are carrying me straight to the top of Mom's Favorite Daughter chart."

"Not fair. You can't use a kid to work your way up the rankings," Hannah grumbled, playing along with the old joke.

Ann sighed and shook her head, looking equally amused and exasperated. "For the hundredth time, I do not have a Favorite Daughter chart. I love you all equally." She turned to Hannah. "How's Fresh doing?"

"Business is great," Hannah replied. "And I'm finally happy with my coconut muffin recipe, so I no longer need to use you guys as guinea pigs."

"Congratulations, dear. You've always been so talented. I knew it wouldn't take you long to perfect the recipe." Ann smoothed a hand down her perfect blond bob and assumed a nonchalant expression. "On another note, I spoke with your brother this morning. He and Sage are working on the seating chart for their wedding reception."

Hannah's wide eyes narrowed a fraction. "So?"

"So, Paxton asked me if you're planning to bring a date. I told him that I'd find out if you're seeing anyone new."

"I work with the public. I see new people all the time."

Claire neutralized a grin behind a cough. She'd known her mom would ask that question to her two single daughters before she'd ever set this lunch up. Heck, she'd counted on it. Claire wasn't known for blurting out personal information, so it would appear way more believable if she told them about dating Ethan only after her mom had peppered her with the usual questions.

"Are any of them eligible, single men?" their mom asked Hannah, a persistent note to her voice.

"No. I'm only attracted to the married ones," Hannah shot back, clearly irritated.

"There's no need for sarcasm. I love you, dear, and I'd simply like to know what's going on in your life."

"I know," Hannah said, her irritation deflating. "I promise to let you know if I start dating someone and to let Pax know if I plan to bring a date to his wedding. Deal?"

"Thank you." Ann accepted the offer graciously before turning to Claire. "How's Ty's soccer going?"

"The coach called an extra team meeting tonight. I'm not sure what that's all about. I guess I'll find out soon enough."

Her mom looked away and fidgeted in her seat. She seemed almost flustered or guilty or something else uncharacteristic of her usual composure. A beat later, Ann returned her gaze and cleared her throat, looking focused once again.

The moment passed so quickly, Claire wondered if she'd imagined it. Why would an upcoming soccer meeting fluster her mom? Aside from being a supportive fan and proud grandma, Ann had no involvement with Ty's team.

"How is Grace enjoying her dance classes and piano lessons?" her mom asked, changing the subject.

"Ballet is still her favorite. Yesterday, she found out she gets to play the part of a magical tear in this year's production of *Tangled.*"

"My, that sounds very important," Ann said proudly. "She's so graceful and naturally talented. I'm sure she'll do a wonderful job. Please forward me the dates and times of her recitals and Ty's soccer matches. Your father and I will plan to attend all of them."

"Send the info my way as well," Kat said. "Logan, Bennett, and I will be there. My niece and nephew are kick-ass at everything they do."

"Agreed," Hannah added with a smile. "I'll be there too."

Love and gratitude warmed her heart. "I'll send their schedules to all of you," Claire said, swallowing back the lump of emotion in her throat. "Thanks. I don't know what the kiddos and I would do without you guys."

"And there'll never be a need to find out." Her mom patted her hand. "Now tell me, dear … " She paused, looking at Claire with hope in her eyes.

Here it comes. The moment when she asked Claire if she was seeing anyone new—the question her mom managed to work into every single conversation. And finally, Claire had an unpredictable, unwise, un-Claire-like response destined to shock them all.

"Yes?" Claire prompted, anxious to announce in a funny-you-should-ask sort of way that, yes, actually she had just started dating someone new—a jobless, smoking-hot young stud who lived with his mother. *Buh-bye, poor, sad, lonely Claire.*

"Are you ready to order?"

Huh? Claire wrinkled her nose and shook her head. Her mom always asked her about men. Always. She looked to her sisters for help, sending a confused look their way.

Kat shrugged. "I like the salads here."

"The quiches are good too," Hannah added, flipping her menu open.

Ugh. She wanted to talk about men, not food. It figured the one time Claire wanted her mom probing into her love life, it didn't happen.

She ran a quick mental diagnostic test, trying to comprehend the situation. Her anxiousness to discuss Ethan must have clouded her judgment. Her mom would likely ask about her dating life once the food arrived. She simply needed to be patient.

For the next hour and a half, they discussed family, friends, work, Pax and Sage's December wedding, and a few other topics Claire would typically find interesting. Today, the conversation chipped away at her patience like a craftsman's chisel on wood. After they settled up the check, her mom picked up her purse and pushed back her chair to leave.

Tapping a beat on the table in frustration, Claire reworked her plan. Sure, it would have been more believable to tell them about Ethan after her mom questioned her, but she had to readjust plans all the time in her job at Bennett Industries. This shouldn't be any different.

She took a calming breath and squared her shoulders. "I almost forgot to mention ..." She paused, waiting until all three sets of eyes were focused on her. "I've started seeing someone."

Her voice shook a little on the lie, but she didn't think they noticed. In fact, her mom and sisters were so busy gawking at Claire, she doubted they'd notice if a flock of aggressive gulls had suddenly started scavenging the table for scraps.

"Seriously?" Kat asked.

"It's more fun than serious." Claire faked a coy smile. "But I have to admit, I like him more than any other man I've met recently, even though he's in his twenties and still lives at his mom's house." Which was all completely true.

Hannah went brows up. "He lives with his mom?"

"He doesn't have a job," Claire explained helpfully.

Ann cocked her head. "He's unemployed and lives at home, and you're attracted to him?"

"Once you see him, you'll understand." She winked and rose from the table. "Thanks for joining me for lunch, ladies. I had a great time."

Her mom and Hannah gaped in wordless wonder, while Kat studied her with an amused smirk.

Before anyone could ask any questions she wasn't ready to answer, Claire strode from the table, pleased with the progression of her plan. She'd laid the groundwork for her relationship with Ethan to accomplish multiple goals over the next two months. Not only would she get out of the auction and prove she didn't need charity to get a date, she'd finally shake off the role of injured little bird in need of help. Nope. After this, she'd be known as a sharp-eyed hawk hunting for young pups to scoop up in her talons.

Okay, that was probably an exaggeration. She grinned to herself, passing through the hotel's double-door entry. But it still felt damn good to take some control back of her personal life.

She slipped on her sunglasses and stepped into the bright August sunshine. Talk about a great return on investment, or a lot of bang for your buck as Kat would say. Her investment in Ethan looked to be the best two grand she'd ever spent.

•••

A few hours later, the click-clacking sound of Claire's peep-toe pumps echoed through the library's two-story foyer as she hurried up the curved stairs. Ty's soccer coach, Josh Klein, had booked one of the conference rooms at the library for the parent-only meeting, and she was late. Again.

As a single mom with a demanding career, Claire knew a thing or two hundred about the intricacies of balancing a jam-packed schedule. Like a house of cards, it only took one miscalculation to bring the whole thing crashing down.

Lunch with her family had meant she'd needed to push back her early afternoon appointment with Bernie Bell, her long-winded head of human resources. Bernie had showed up at her office at four o'clock, promising to only take a few minutes of her time, then proceeded to vent about his staff's incompetence for over an hour. The moment Claire had finally shooed him from her office, she'd raced to her car and sped through a few orange-ish stoplights, keeping an eye on the darkening sky overhead.

While she'd managed to make it inside the library before the impending summer storm hit, she'd arrived five minutes *after* the soccer meeting's start time.

She checked her watch again and hurried down the long corridor. She glanced in each conference-room doorway as she rushed by, hoping to find the team before Coach Klein started talking.

At the third room, her heels stuttered to a stop on the slick tile. Inside, a tall, muscular guy stood near the whiteboard, lighting up the room with a thousand-watt smile. Recognition and stupefaction hit her with the old one-two.

"Ethan?" she squeaked.

Thumbs tucked casually in the pockets of his jeans, he turned to her. "Evening, Claire," he said, looking way happier to see her than she was to see him. "Come on in and take a seat. We were waiting for you to get started."

Mouth agape, her fingertips tingling, she heard a rush of white noise in her ears. Her pulse kicked into frantic overdrive. *No, no, no, no, no.* Her fake boyfriend couldn't be here for her son's soccer meeting. No way would the universe be that cruel.

Ethan encouraged her into the room with a cute little wave. "Don't be scared. I don't bite." He winked.

His teasing comment set off a chorus of laughter. Though Claire couldn't see far into the room from where she stood in the hallway, it sounded like every single one of the team's parents had beat her to the meeting. *Terrific.*

Without thinking, she let her wayward feet carry her inside. Once she cleared the doorway, approximately twenty-five sets of eyes blasted her with amused interest.

"Sorry I'm late," she mumbled, fighting the blush creeping up her neck as she slid into a back-row seat.

"No problem," Coach Klein said, stepping forward, his round face flushed and beaming with pleasure. "I'm just glad everyone was able to make it tonight for the big announcement."

What announcement?

Slouched in her chair and fighting back rising anxiety, Claire peeked through her fingers at the surreal scene at the front of the room.

Coach Klein continued, "Unless you've been living under a rock, I'm sure you all recognize the amazing man next to me, the greatest athlete to ever come out of Silver Bay, our very own Ethan DuBois."

The room exploded in thunderous applause and whoops of excitement.

Claire reeled back as recognition slammed into her. She'd heard Ty talk about the soccer star before. And way before that, when she'd still been in college on the East Coast, she remembered her mom talking about a high school soccer player from Silver Bay who'd made the national team.

"While Ethan takes a … " Coach Klein paused and cleared his throat. " … a break from soccer, he's generously volunteered to coach a local youth team for the season. I'm thrilled to announce the club has made him head coach of our boys' team!" He pumped his fist in victory as another deafening wave of applause swept through the room.

Claire's stomach dropped, and her face caught fire. Oh. Holy. Smokes. She'd propositioned the town's favorite son and her kid's new soccer coach.

Her gaze flew to Ethan's in pained accusation as the commotion carried on around them. The jerk had purposely let her believe he was some slacker with no direction in life.

To his credit, Ethan looked back with a hesitant half-smile and an apologetic tilt to his eyebrows rather than full-out mocking amusement. He mouthed the word "surprise" in that anticlimactic way people do when they know damn well the person they're surprising is so *not* going to like the flipping surprise.

Thankfully, Coach Klein pulled Ethan's attention away from her a moment later.

Sinking lower and leaning to the left, Claire managed to hide behind the tall father of the team's goalie for the remaining thirty minutes of the meeting. Too proud—or maybe too stupid—to run for cover, she even mingled with a few parents afterward, all-the-while avoiding Ethan. She needed time to smooth the jagged-edged embarrassment slicing through her before dealing with the jerk.

She silently cursed her sister's stupid bachelorette auction. Maybe she should have swallowed her pride and stood on that blasted stage like an idiot. Instead, she'd tried to find a business solution to a personal problem. Big flipping mistake.

He must have found her offer to 'buy' his services hilarious. Glaring at Ethan's back and ridiculously wide shoulders from across the room, she ground her teeth and drew in a long, slow breath. Rather than clarify the misunderstanding, he'd let her believe he was a goalless pretty boy who needed cash.

Her embarrassment began to morph into anger. The more she thought about it, the more she fumed. He'd played her to perfection.

Ugh. She'd even offered him a cash advance in case he didn't have enough money to pay for a date with her. A big-time pro soccer player probably made more money in one endorsement deal than she did all year at Bennett Industries.

Wanting to cringe or growl or punch something, she had another thought occur to her. Ethan had been interested in her father and her kids' ages the night she'd offered to buy his services. Had he put two and two together? Had he figured out he'd be coaching her son's team and not flipping told her?

"Bastard," she growled under her breath, her pulse pounding in her ears. The startled looks around her jolted her into action. "Custard," she improvised. "Just remembered I need to buy custard on the way home. Gotta go," she mumbled to no one in particular and slipped from the room.

She bolted down the stairs, not even slowing when she saw the torrential rainfall pounding down outside. Welcoming the onslaught, she burst through the front door and raced into the downpour to the safety and seclusion of her SUV.

Soaked and dripping all over her car's leather interior, she slammed her door closed and indulged in a few self-indulgent forehead thunks against her steering wheel.

A moment later, three firm knocks against her side window startled her upright. She swiveled her head so quickly to the left her wet hair whipped across the headrest. Ethan stood outside her car, looking unfazed at the assault of horizontal rain.

He blasted her with his spellbinding smile. "We need to talk," he mouthed through the closed window.

"Go away." Claire angrily gestured in the other direction.

"Can't hear you in this storm," he yelled. "I'll join you in there."

Aghast, she watched him jog around the front of her car. Before she had the sense to hit the locks, he slid into the passenger seat.

"Sorry to soak your car," he said, slicking his hair back from his face. "I forgot how quickly storms blow in around here."

"I'd worry less about my car's interior and more about me strangling you." Claire squinted through the water cascading down her windshield. "Do you think the fog on the windows will provide enough cover? Or could somebody still see me murdering you?"

"Upset I didn't tell you the other night?"

She narrowed her eyes, shooting him a don't-be-an-idiot look.

"I'll take that as a yes. Would it have changed anything?"

"Absolutely. Deal's off."

He went brows up. "You're firing me? Again?"

"You lied to me."

His expression soured. "I never lied."

"You let me think you were an unemployed pretty boy who lived with his mother."

"I told you I was retired. Which I am," he said. "Even if no one wants to believe me," he added under his breath. "And I didn't say I lived with my mother. I said I lived in her guest room, which is true. Mom hasn't moved into the house yet. So it made sense for me to stay there."

"If it's her house, why hasn't she moved in?" Claire snapped.

An almost imperceptible tension tightened his face. "Long story." But he didn't elaborate.

She studied him, staring into the depths of those gorgeous blue eyes, trying to work out what he wasn't telling her. He locked gazes with her. For once, his eyes burned with heated intensity rather than good-natured humor.

The air pressure shifted. A growing awareness of him hummed through her, and the car seemed to shrink. The fogged windows and the blinding rain of the summer storm brought an unexpected intimacy to the enclosed space.

"Ethan." It was meant as a warning, but her throaty whisper sounded more like a plea. She licked her lips and gave her head a small shake, trying to clear the sensual haze from her mind.

His gaze dropped to her mouth. "Claire."

Her name on his lips was neither a plea nor a warning. His voice held only confident intent. He slowly stroked his thumb down her jawline and across her sensitive lower lip, his eyes darkening with desire.

Her heart pounded in her chest as every nerve ending in her body came alive. *Oh God.* He wanted to kiss her.

He played you for a fool. He played you for a fool. He played you for a fool.

By the third repeat, the depressing anti-pep talk roared through her head and broke the spell. Claire clenched her teeth and leaned away from his touch—both frustrated by and thankful for her maturity.

"Nice try at seduction, but you still lied." She kept her voice as neutral as possible under the circumstances. "And you're still fired."

FOUR

ETHAN effortlessly juggled the soccer ball from thigh to foot and back to thigh again. While August afternoons in Wisconsin could be hot and humid, today a cool breeze blew off of the lake, tempering the late summer sun. Based off the laughter coming from the group of ten-year-old boys he'd been coaching for two weeks, his team liked the reprieve from heat as much as he did.

"Remember, guys, you have to complete twenty-five juggles during warm-ups before shooting on the goal."

That earned him a few groans from his team. Smiling at the predictable reaction, he dropped the ball to the ground and did a quick head count. Claire's son, Ty, hadn't arrived yet, which meant she hadn't arrived either.

Before he could even finish the thought, her silver, high-end SUV turned into the complex and rolled to a stop by the practice field. Ty bolted from the passenger seat and ran to join his team. Smart and dedicated, he exemplified everything Ethan could want in a player.

"Hi, Coach," Ty said with a big grin as he dropped his bag and immediately started warming up.

"Hey, Ty. Have you been working on the extra drills I showed you last practice?"

"Yeah, they're lit! Mom said I look like a pro doing the Maradona."

"Great," Ethan said, smiling at Ty's youthful enthusiasm.

Naturally talented, Claire's son also focused more and worked harder than any other player at practice. If Ty maintained that work ethic and signed up for some additional training over the next few years, he could develop into an exceptional regional player.

Of course, having full parental support behind that goal would help Ty tremendously. Ethan looked toward the parking lot, wondering if Claire understood soccer could be more than just a recreational sport for her son. And if she knew, did she care? Not all parents approved of making soccer a priority.

Maybe he could talk to her about Ty?

He watched Claire lower her bike from a rack hanging on the back of her SUV. At the end of practice, he knew he'd watch her load it back on the rack, like he did at every practice. She still hadn't spoken to him since firing him—for the second damn time.

If she hadn't called off their arrangement, tonight would have been their first date at Bayside. Ethan had to admit that he was a little thrown by her rejection. He looked down at the soccer ball in front of him and stepped into it with his right foot. The ball rocketed past the team and into the back corner of the net. His players whooped in appreciation. If only he could impress Claire so easily.

He couldn't remember the last time he'd had to work at impressing a woman. Hell, women generally chased *him*. He'd been asked out via social media more times than he could remember. Even his last few girlfriends had approached him first, either directly or indirectly, through mutual friends. Not so surprisingly, they'd all turned out to be clingy, needy, and way more interested in his celebrity status as a professional athlete than in him as an actual person.

The fact that Claire seemed both underwhelmed and immune, provided an interesting change and an irresistible challenge. And when had he not been up for a challenge?

He turned toward the parking lot again. Instead of Claire biking her cute butt out of the park, she stood motionless, staring directly at him with a gaze hot enough to start a fire. Maybe she wasn't as immune as she pretended to be.

Ethan felt a slow, predatory smile spread across his face. He raised his head in a cocky nod of both greeting and acknowledgement of her inspection. When she shook her head in a nearly imperceptible warning, adrenaline pumped through him. His smile widened in silent acceptance of her challenge.

Winning over the reserved, beautiful Claire Bennett might not be an easy goal to achieve, but he'd made a career out of making goals others deemed impossible.

First things first. They'd need to spend time together if he wanted her to warm up to him. And what better way to spend time together than going on a few dates—pretend or otherwise?

Time to get unfired.

•••

Crap. Double crap. Ethan had caught her staring at him. Cheeks burning, Claire shoved her phone and car keys into the small cargo bag attached to her bike. Why did she always embarrass herself around that man?

"We probably used up a lifetime's worth of luck the day Ethan DuBois got placed as the team's coach," a raspy voice observed behind her. Grinning, Deb Saunders, her friend and biking companion, pulled her bike to a stop beside Claire. "I feel like we won the lottery."

"A more powerful force than luck intervened," Claire explained. "Apparently, once my dad heard about Ethan, he made a few well-placed phone calls to ensure his grandson's team had the honor of being led by Silver Bay's finest athlete."

"Your dad rocks."

Claire snorted. "He has his moments."

Deb stuffed her curly blond hair inside her bike helmet, adjusted her bike shorts over her eye-catching curves, and gave Ethan a little wave. Happily married and outgoing, Deb interacted with him with ease.

Claire fastened her helmet and jammed her water bottle in the holder. "Ready to go? I don't want Ty to think I'm spying on practice."

"Bull. You don't want Ethan to know you're watching him. I still can't believe you thought he was my cousin." Deb chuckled.

Claire scrunched her eyes closed and squeezed the bridge of her nose. "Can we not relive that moment?"

"You really should have taken him up on his offer to help."

Claire dropped her hand with a sigh and focused on Deb. "I couldn't once I found out who he really was."

"Why not?"

"He lied to me," Claire said. "Besides, he doesn't need the money, so why'd he agree to help?" She shook her head. "I don't do business with people unless I understand their motives."

"Sex is a pretty strong motivator." Deb waggled her eyebrows. "Maybe he was hoping to get some."

"Please." Claire rolled her eyes. "He probably has female sportscasters and Hollywood It girls on speed dial. Why would he bother pursuing a small-town mom with a reputation duller than a pair of safety scissors?"

"You're not dull. You're classy. There's a big difference," Deb insisted, sounding offended on Claire's behalf.

"Thanks, Deb." Claire was appreciative of her friend's glass-half-full opinion. "Now can we go? At this rate, practice is going to be over before we even start our ride."

"Good point. If we don't hurry, we'll miss Ethan leading the cooldown stretches. That's one of my favorite parts." With a determined look, Deb hopped on her bike and pushed off toward the bike path.

Claire caught up and settled into pace by her side, glad of the comfortable silence on these rides. The last thing she wanted to do was talk more about her inconvenient attraction to Ethan.

Eager to clear her mind of her son's coach, she shifted gears and pedaled past Deb. As she pushed the bike, the sound of it whizzing along mingled with the laughter of children in the park's playground. The intricate designs of the gardens and the passing trees blurred into a kaleidoscope of color in her peripheral vision. Her breathing deepened; her focus narrowed to the path ahead.

She maintained the grueling pace until she reached a shaded bench beside the trail that overlooked a bend in the creek. Sweating, panting, legs shaking, she pulled to the side and reached for her water, waiting for Deb to catch up.

"Holy hell, lady." Her friend panted to a stop next to her a minute later. "I haven't ridden that fast since I tried to ditch the twins during our family bike ride three weeks ago." She paused to take two large gulps from her water bottle, then leveled Claire with an inquisitive look. "What's up?"

Claire turned to look at the creek. "Nothing. It just felt good to let off some steam."

"Sex is a hell of a lot better way to let off steam," Deb mumbled. "You've gotta start getting some, or I'm quitting these rides. They hired a new cop in town. I've seen him getting coffee at Fresh most mornings. He's tall, blond, and all kinds of hot. Plus, you can't go wrong with a guy who really knows how to work a pair of handcuffs."

"Don't start," Claire warned. "I've told you, I'll date when I want to and not because some hunk with an expertise in restraints moves to town."

"Fine. If you don't want to talk about your real love life, then let's discuss your fake one." Deb glanced at her watch. "We have a few minutes before heading back to practice. Fill me in on whatever new plan you're concocting to get out of the auction. Are

47

you going to pay someone else to squire you around town? Maybe send away for a mail-order husband? Or maybe you could try something really crazy," Deb said dryly, "and simply take part in the auction, go on one silly date, and put the thing behind you."

"You were in my fourth-grade class. Remember what happened last time I was super nervous on stage?" Claire faked a heave.

"I don't buy it." Deb looked skeptical. "You're an exec at Bennett. You speak in front of people all the time."

"That's totally different," Claire countered. "That's business. I don't get nervous conducting business. But standing on stage in front of the entire town, including my ex-husband, looking desperate and pathetic." She turned her head from side to side, slow and emphatic. "No way."

"Fine." Deb held up her hands in surrender. "What's your new plan?"

Claire blew out a breath. "I haven't come up with one yet." She looked hopefully at Deb. "Any chance your cousin is back on the market and looking to make some extra cash?"

"Nope. He's bringing Roberta over next Sunday for a cookout. He thinks she may be the one."

"The one?" Claire jerked back. "Didn't he just meet her?"

"Yeah. Seems quick to me too." Deb shrugged. "Oh well. Who am I to question love at first sight?"

Claire gave a mental eye roll and rubbed the heart-shaped pendant around her neck. She used to believe in love at first sight and happily-ever-afters. She'd even been known as the family romantic once upon a time. But for her, true love didn't exist in the passionate embrace of a lover. True love lived in the pure, unconditional love she felt for her children.

And that was enough for her.

"Time to head back to practice," she said, climbing onto her bike.

"Good point. They're probably doing the cooldown stretches."

"No catcalls this time," Claire warned, setting off at a slower pace for the return ride. "I honestly thought Ethan might ban you from practice last week."

"Not my fault. He stripped off his sweatshirt."

"You yelled for him to 'take it all off,' twice."

"What was I supposed to do?"

"Say nothing?" Claire suggested.

Deb's eyebrows dipped in confusion. "That's no fun."

"True." Claire grinned. "But it's mature and responsible."

"Being mature and responsible sounds kinda boring."

Unable to argue the point, Claire let the conversation drift to silence as they finished their ride back to the soccer field.

"This is better than I could have ever imagined," Deb yelled over her shoulder to Claire and hopped off her bike to watch the last few minutes of practice.

Claire brought her bike to a stop and looked to the field.

Holy smokes.

Ethan had joined the end-of-practice scrimmage on the skins' side. Broad shoulders, washboard abs, and powerful legs filled her vision. He moved with a mesmerizing combination of power, grace, and testosterone. Her heartbeat pounded in avid appreciation. She tried to look away and failed.

Transfixed, she continued to watch the boys race up and down the field, their faces lit with youthful joy as they played the game they loved. Ethan appeared to be having a great time too, hustling, jostling, and laughing as much as the rest of the players.

"If Mike took Pilates, do you think his abs would look like that?"

Claire turned her gaze from the male paragon on the field to take in her friend's wistful expression.

Oh boy.

Deb's husband, Mike, managed the local grocery store, spent most of his day under florescent lighting, and was rumored to polish off the day-old bakery items during his break time. He had a big heart, friendly smile, and a body more reminiscent of a professional bowler than a soccer star. Should she be honest or should she be nice?

Who was she kidding? A crusher of dreams, she was not—best to avoid answering the question directly. "Mike is great. He loves you and the boys more than anything. That's better than perfect abs."

Deb blew out a sigh. "Yeah. The only six-pack in Mike's future is the one he brings home from the store every Friday night."

Thankfully, Ethan called an end to practice, saving Claire from a further discussion of Mike's doughy body.

While most of the boys began gathering their bags and gear to head home, she hauled Ty's sleepover stuff to Deb's minivan. Ty, as usual, lingered on the field to ask Ethan some soccer-based question.

She watched as he paid rapt attention to his coach's response. A wave of gratitude slammed into her. She wondered if Ethan knew her son had already elevated him to a near godly status.

Claire found herself walking toward them. Her body seemed as drawn to Ethan as her eyes. She'd cut the distance between them in half when Ethan ruffled Ty's blond hair and shot him a smile, the corners of his eyes crinkling. Ty beamed back, then hurried to his soccer bag to switch from cleats to street shoes.

At the same moment that Claire realized she was standing in the middle of the soccer field for no apparent reason, Ethan looked up and caught her staring at him. Again.

Ugh.

His smile amped up to its full thousand watts. "Hey."

She quickly scooped up a plastic bottle discarded by one of the players, desperate for an excuse to be standing there. She waved it around with a little too much enthusiasm. "Just picking up some litter."

Could she sound any more ridiculous? She usually prided herself on her quick thinking and easy banter. Like lightening striking a computer, Ethan's hotness must have fried the area of her brain responsible for logical communication.

"Mom!" Ty charged up beside her before Ethan could comment on her sudden interest in soccer-field cleanliness. "Could you take my soccer bag home? I don't want to take it to Rhys and Aidan's house for the sleepover."

"Sure, kiddo. I already put your sleeping bag and duffle in their car." She swung his backpack onto her shoulder and pulled him in for a big hug. "Be good for Ms. Deb. Go to bed at a decent hour, and remember to brush your teeth."

"I will. I love you, Mom! Bye!"

"Bye, kiddo. I love you too," she said to herself. Ty had already sprinted off to join his friends.

Claire turned and hustled back to her car, hoping to avoid any more embarrassing interactions with Ethan. When would she get over this annoying physical attraction? Maybe Deb was right. Maybe she did need to get some. With a half snort, half grunt, and a full eye roll at her pathetic lack of a sex life, she tossed Ty's bag onto the backseat and moved to the back of her SUV to load her bike.

The air suddenly thickened. Only one guy could make her body go on high alert simply by being near.

"Let me help you." Ethan's voice sent a shiver of awareness down her spine. Before she realized his intentions, he moved forward to pick up her bike, and his hand inadvertently brushed her arm.

Claire jumped back with a small squeak as electricity shot up her arm and quickly headed south.

With her bike suspended in midair, Ethan looked over his shoulder. "Are you okay?"

"Yup. Dandy."

Dandy? Nobody under the age of sixty said dandy.

She looked down, as if she found the piece of gum stuck on the pavement a few feet away incredibly interesting. Thankfully, the wind blowing her hair across her face hid the blush she could feel all the way to her hairline. She needed another minute to get control before her red cheeks would subside.

Sheesh. She'd blushed more around Ethan than she had in years.

"I think something flew into my eye," she lied, wiping her eye in a pretend effort to remove the pretend object.

"Let me take a look." Ethan put his hand under her chin, leaned in close, and thoroughly examined the eye she'd been fiddling with. "Hmmm," he hummed low in his throat. "I don't see anything."

His breath on her face sent another ripple of awareness through her. He must have sensed her response because he looked hard into her eyes—but no longer in an effort to find a stray eyelash. His lips curved in a sexy smile that engaged his dimples.

He dropped his hand from her chin and straightened, not stepping back. "Have dinner with me tonight."

"No," she said, a bit too quickly in retrospect.

He cocked his head and studied her with a teasing light in his eyes. "Is it too short notice to find a sitter?"

"It's not that. Ty's sleeping at Rhys and Aidan's house tonight, and my sister Hannah asked Grace over to binge watch *MasterChef.*"

"Then why not have dinner with me?"

"Because you're my son's soccer coach. That's the extent of our relationship." The words sounded so logical. So reasonable. Why couldn't her body get the message?

"This is about soccer." His hypnotic smile returned. "I'd like to talk to you about an opportunity for Ty."

"So this would be a meeting between coach and parent?" Claire narrowed her eyes at him.

"Something like that. Seven at Bayside?"

She stared at him for a long, heavy beat—well aware he'd just suggested they go to dinner on the exact same day and at the exact same time and location of the date she'd planned for them before firing him. "I'll only go if you agree it's a soccer meeting, not a date."

"Let's compromise and call it a soccer date." He winked. "See you tonight."

Eyes wide, Claire watched Ethan stride toward his Jeep, hands in his pockets, whistling an off-key, carefree tune. Had she just agreed to go out with him? Damn. She knew he was a world-class striker, able to blow past defenders with ease. She hadn't realized his abilities carried to off-the-field situations as well.

She wouldn't kid herself into believing a pro-athlete was seriously interested in dating a small-town single mom. The guy must hit on every woman he met if he was putting this much effort into going out with her.

She needed to put a stop to whatever he was up to before it went any further. She'd amp up her defenses, meet Ethan for dinner, and make it crystal clear to the thick-headed Adonis that he needed to move on to the next girl in line because their relationship would never advance beyond the parent-to-coach level.

The simplicity of the plan pleased her. As long as she kept her cool and maintained focus on her goal, Claire felt confident nothing could go wrong.

FIVE

EXACTLY fifteen minutes before his date with Claire, Ethan pulled his Jeep into a parking spot directly in front of Bayside, the town's best bar and grill. Like most of the popular businesses in town, Bayside sat on one of the four streets circling Sullivan Square—or the Square, as everyone referred to it.

Since Ethan had moved from Silver Bay, the town had poured money into making the Square an appealing destination for locals and a growing number of tourists. Two blocks long and one block wide, it represented small-town Wisconsin at its finest. Old-fashioned street lamps, wide sidewalks with brick accents, planters full of bright flowers, and small trees with twinkling lights lined the streets.

Bayside was located in a brown brick building on the northwest corner. With an interior with more brick, dark wood, and multiple wide windows, the restaurant had an upscale pub atmosphere and great food that had made it a Silver Bay institution.

Ethan slid into a booth in the bar area along the wall of windows. Outside, couples of all ages strolled by, hand-in-hand. Moms pushed strollers, dads carried toddlers, and teenagers lounged on the benches dotting the pedestrian-only blocks across the street.

Nostalgia tightened his chest. When he moved from Silver Bay to Los Angeles after high school, he'd assumed he'd spend the rest of his life in some urban location, enjoying the big-city attractions Silver Bay lacked. At the time, he hadn't appreciated the charm and camaraderie of small-town life.

Distance had brought clarity. Silver Bay didn't have any professional sports teams, Michelin-star restaurants, or all-night dance clubs, but it did offer a place to live where you could feel connected to and vested in a welcoming community. Even after living elsewhere for so long, Silver Bay felt like home to Ethan. It probably always would.

Continuing to look out the window, he spotted Claire a block away, her efficient stride carrying her through the locals and tourists. She occasionally nodded in greeting as she worked her way through the Friday night crowd.

When she stepped through the door, a shot of adrenaline hit his system. Her blond hair was loose, the straight, thick strands brushing her shoulders. Her fitted white blouse, heeled sandals, and dark denim jeans lengthened and narrowed her slender build.

As their eyes met, he stood up and smiled. "Thanks for joining me for dinner. I'm a *lucky* guy to have such a beautiful date."

She sighed and squared her shoulders, her expression a cross between determination and resignation. Flirting didn't look to be on her agenda tonight. Which, of course, only made him want to do it more.

"Ethan," she said with a nod, her tight voice making his name sound like an obstacle to overcome.

Good thing he loved a challenge. He fought a grin and gestured for her to take a seat.

She slid into the opposite side of the booth and scanned the room. Her body radiated tension as her fingers tapped out a nervous beat on the weathered, wooden table-top.

"You okay?" he asked.

Her focus snapped to him. "This is a very visible table. Anyone inside or outside the restaurant will see us together."

"A couple of weeks ago, you wanted to show me off around town as your new boyfriend. Now you're embarrassed to be seen with me." He shook his head in exaggerated disappointment. "I feel like I just got cut from the team."

"You'll survive," she said, sounding half amused and half exasperated. "I'm trying to avoid people getting the wrong idea. I plan to make sure *everyone* knows we're only here to discuss soccer."

"Yep. I remember. We're on a soccer date."

"No. Not a date. Just a meeting to talk about soccer. Besides, there's no such thing as a soccer date."

"Sure, there is," he countered with enthusiasm. "It's what we're doing right now. Going on a date to discuss soccer."

Claire opened her mouth to respond at the same moment a college-aged waiter stopped at their table.

"Can I bring you something to drink?"

"I'll have a water," Claire announced in a voice loud enough to address the entire bar. "I'm not going to have any alcohol because my son's coach and I are only here to discuss soccer."

The waiter eyed her in confusion. "Ohhh-kaaay." He turned to Ethan. "How about you?"

"I'll stick with beer." He looked at Claire. "It's the perfect drink for a soccer date."

She gave her head a slight exasperated shake. When the waiter left to get their drinks, she added, "You're trouble."

He responded with his most charming smile. "Yeah. But I'm worth it."

She tipped her head to study him with her beautiful blue, green, and gold-flecked eyes. The position exposed an expanse of pale skin along her neck that begged to be licked, kissed, and nipped. Could she taste as sweet as she looked? He swallowed hard. Damn, he wasn't sure anyone could taste that good.

"That's what I hear," she said, looking amused. "You're the talk of the town. Is Silver Bay's unending supply of adoring fans the reason you moved back here instead of staying in Chicago? As far as amenities go, it's hard for us to compete with what a big city can offer."

"I don't know about that. From where I sit, *you*"—he emphasized the word—"have a lot to offer a guy."

"Good point. *Silver Bay*"—she mimicked his emphasis—"is no longer all about fishing and lumber."

"That's right. Bennett Industries started as a lumber mill."

"Yeah. When my father took over the business from my grandfather, he began transitioning to cabinets. He knew profits would soar by moving from selling a commodity to selling a finished product. We're now adding a furniture line."

"Smart man."

"He's done well."

"Do you work with him?" Ethan asked.

"Yeah. I take care of whatever Dad needs me to handle on any given day."

"Sounds interesting."

"Surprisingly, it is. After college, he offered me the position until I found something I liked better." She shrugged. "Turns out, I really enjoy my job, and I'm pretty good at it."

When their waiter returned with their drinks, Claire ordered a bowl of soup and a salad for her dinner. Ethan added a steak sandwich to the order and bided his time until they were alone.

"I haven't met Ty's dad yet. Does he come to any of his son's games?" Bringing up an ex-husband was the equivalent of playing soccer in a torrential downpour—no matter how careful he tried to be, odds were good he'd slip and fall on his ass at some point.

The corners of her full mouth turned down. "Jack travels for work, so he only makes it to a few games per season."

"What's he do?"

"He sells drugs."

Ethan blinked. "Not going to lie." He shook his head slowly from side to side. "I didn't see that one coming."

She grinned. "To be fair, the drugs are legal. He's a pharmaceutical sales rep. Which means he spends his time pitching the benefits of his drugs to doctors."

"Ahhh." Ethan leaned back in the booth. "That makes more sense. I can't see you with a drug dealer." He squinted his eyes, feigning contemplation. "Although, I did mistake you for a hooker when we met."

"What?" she squeaked.

"I only thought it for a little bit." He held his thumb and forefinger about an inch apart. "Then I realized you were only interested in procuring services, not offering 'em."

Claire's mouth dropped open and her beautiful eyes went wide. Then she dropped her head back and laughed—a full, rich, sexy-as-hell laugh that kicked off a rush of desire.

His gaze dropped to the curve of her exposed neck, and then—while her head was still tipped to the ceiling—he snuck a look at the rounded swell of her breasts wrapped snuggly in the silky-looking fabric of her top. Damn, she had great breasts. They looked high and firm and big enough to fill his hands if he held them.

No, scratch that. Not *if* he held them—*when* he held them.

He tore his gaze from her chest as she lowered her head to look at him again. The instant her warm, inviting laugh tapered off, he wanted to hear it again. He wanted to make her happy—very happy. A vivid picture flashed through his mind: her wrapped around his body, half undressed and laughing as they stumbled through a bedroom doorway together.

He went hard.

Shit. Ethan gritted his teeth. He felt like a frigging teenager, getting aroused over a throaty laugh, completely covered breasts, and his own vivid imagination.

"Sorry." She wiped a stray tear from the corner of her eye and took two deep breaths, obviously fighting to suppress more laughter. "I haven't laughed that hard in ages. The closest I've ever come to being mistaken for a lady of the night was the time Kat told me my new heels were *F*-me shoes." She wet her lower lip. "They've been buried in the back of my closet ever since."

"Sounds like you need a second opinion." He gave her a wolfish look. "How about you wear them on our next date, and I'll let you know what they say to me?"

"Sorry, Lucky, there will be no more dates, soccer or otherwise."

He cocked an eyebrow. "Have you already hired my replacement?"

She cleared her throat and glanced out the window before answering. "The position is proving harder to fill than I originally anticipated."

"My offer still stands," he said, attempting to appear both friendly and harmless.

He must have overdone the innocent bit because she narrowed her eyes, looking skeptical. "Why?" she eventually asked. "Why are you willing to do this? It's not for the money. Obviously."

"You—"

"No." Claire held up her hand to interrupt. "We barely know each other. I don't buy that you'd do this simply to help out a person you've just met. And no BS reason—like my charming personality has inspired you to play the role of Good Samaritan." She leaned forward, all business now. "What is *your* reason for helping me? What would *you* get out of this?"

He pondered how best to answer. Would admitting he wanted her in his bed help or hurt his chances of getting her there? While he had no intention of deceiving her, he didn't want to scare her off by bringing up sex on their sort of first date.

"I enjoy spending time with you." He shrugged a shoulder. "I'd like to do it more." Ethan leaned back and stretched one arm along the top of the booth, pleased with his diplomatic response.

Claire's eyes shifted to his bicep. A beat later, she dropped her gaze, licked her lips, and fidgeted in her seat. Satisfaction uncurled through him. She had more tells than a team of rookie players in their first shootout. Her body language couldn't be clearer. She wanted him too.

Time to press his advantage.

"Think about it, Claire. I'm your way out of the auction. And I'll even do it for free."

Looking even more skeptical, she toyed with the heart-shaped pendant on her necklace and scrutinized him with her penetrating eyes. "I have to pay someone, or it won't be a business deal."

"You can donate my two-grand salary to the charity. Everyone wins."

She turned her head from side-to-side, clearly suspicious. "Why would a man who has his pick of women work so hard to spend time with one?"

He held up his hands in an I've-got-no-tricks-up-my-sleeve gesture. "Everything I've told you is true."

"I'm more interested in everything you're *not* telling me. With you, those seem to be the most interesting details."

"It's our first date—"

"Soccer meeting," she interrupted.

"It's our first soccer date," he corrected. "You can't expect me to give up all my secrets. Just think about it," he added quickly before she could correct him again. "I'm happy to help."

Claire studied him a moment longer, then dipped her head in acceptance. "Okay. I'll think about it."

The progress—albeit slow—pleased him.

Their dinners arrived, and Claire placed her napkin in her lap. "Now tell me … " She sat forward in the booth, her expression all business. "What did you want to discuss about Ty's soccer training?"

Ethan found himself wanting her to approve of his proposed training for her son. He liked Claire. Being with her was the perfect mix of sexual awareness and playful banter. It felt natural. It felt right. And it would suck if she thought his suggestion was shit.

"I see a lot of potential in Ty. I know of an additional training opportunity he could benefit from."

"Fill me in."

"I think Ty should try out for ODP, the Olympic Development Program." He eyed her for a reaction, but her expression remained neutral. "Making the team would give him a chance to train with more advanced, dedicated players than he can play with here. I think it could be a great stepping-stone for him."

"Do you know the details of the program?" she asked, sounding like the businesswoman he knew her to be.

"He'd still play on his team here. This would be

an additional commitment. It's more expensive and would take a lot more hours out of your month than his local training."

As they ate, he went over costs and explained the approximate time commitment required to participate. Even though Claire paid close attention and jotted down notes, her expression remained neutral.

Damn. Was a mom showing excitement or pride in her son's soccer ability too much to ask?

She slipped her notes into her purse. "Thanks for the info. It's great to hear you think so much of Ty. I'll talk to him and let you know his decision soon."

When the waiter returned to clear the table, Claire declined dessert and asked for the check. "We can split it," she insisted.

Ethan wasn't splitting anything. While he waited to pay, her comment about Ty kept playing through his mind. In his experience, moms didn't willingly let their kids make any significant decisions in life.

"So, you plan to let Ty decide about the soccer training? I thought you'd want final say."

Claire shook her head. "He's the one who'll have to put in the extra hours and extra effort. It has to be his decision." She took a sip of water and looked out the window. "For what it's worth, I think it sounds like a good idea."

A feeling of warmth unspooled inside him. It wasn't desire or even attraction. It felt more like ... affection. For Claire. From what he could tell, she loved and supported her kids without condition.

Yep. He'd known from the moment he'd met her that Claire Bennett epitomized class and grace.

Roughly two seconds later, the epitome of class and grace sitting across from him let loose a string of swear words that would have made his rough-around-the-edges former coach take notice. She twisted her head sharply away from the window, looking as if she were desperately trying to hide her face from someone outside.

"Problem?" he drawled.

Before she could answer, he heard an enthusiastic knock on the glass. More than a little curious, he turned to see who wanted their attention.

"Don't look!" she hissed.

"Too late." Ethan was already studying the slightly mismatched couple staring at them through the window.

The tall, brown-haired guy wore a confused, tight-lipped expression on his face. Ethan wasn't sure if it was the gray around the dude's temples or his pissy expression, but he looked at least ten years older than the short, bubbly, curvaceous, and unnaturally tan twenty-something brunette with him.

"Yoo-hoo, Claire!" the girl shouted through the glass, waving enthusiastically. "Can you hear me?" She tilted her head in confusion. "Is this glass, like, soundproof?" she yelled, then started knocking again.

"Sorry to say, pretending you don't see her is only making her more frantic." Ethan tried not to laugh. "Besides, once she realizes everybody else in the place is staring at her, she's going to figure out the glass isn't soundproof."

Claire whimpered a painful sound of resignation and slowly turned toward the window. She gave the girl a small wave and an unconvincing smile. "Hi,

Gemma."

"OMG!" The bubbly brunette bounced up and down, clapping her hands. "I can't believe you're having dinner with Ethan DuBois!" One hand beside her mouth, as if she could actually share a secret screaming through the window of a restaurant, she whisper-yelled, "I think he's gorgeous." Then she dropped her hand and turned to look at Ethan. "I think you're gorgeous!" She clapped her hands again. "Eee! Scoot over. We're coming in to join you!" She grabbed the arm of the pissy-faced dude, who looked even pissier now, and started dragging him toward the entrance.

Claire groaned and rubbed her fingertips in circles over her temples. She glanced in the opposite direction, as if considering escape.

"Don't even think about it. You can't leave me alone with that heaping spoonful of crazy."

She blew out a sigh. "Fine. I'll stay," she said, her tone full of stoic resignation.

"Friends of yours?" he asked, glancing over to see the couple step through Bayside's front door.

"Not quite," she mumbled. "He's my ex-husband, and Gemma's the wife he always wanted."

SIX

IGNORING the flash of surprise on Ethan's face, Claire braced herself for Gemma's flamboyant arrival. Her back to the door, Claire could hear the younger woman's high-pitched voice and the clack, clack, clack of her ever-present stiletto heels, which were closing in on them like two heat-seeking missiles.

Three. Two. One.

"Scoochy, scoochy," Gemma singsonged, gesturing for Claire to move over so she could join her in the booth. "I'm so glad I saw you. I've been really, like *really*, wanting to talk to you."

Claire scooted over and Gemma sat down, her eyes lit with excitement.

When Jack had first dumped Claire and married the younger, perky Gemma less than a year later, Claire had assumed she'd dislike the girl and that, in turn, the girl would forever dislike her. From day one, however, Gemma had treated Claire more like an older, wiser sister than the ex-wife of her new husband. The bizarro relationship made Claire uneasy. Either Gemma didn't notice or didn't care.

"Sorry I haven't replied to your texts, Gemma. I've been busy."

"No sweat. I know you're super good at your job and the world's best mom. I just really wanted to tell you our exciting news!"

Claire forced a smile, not sure she wanted to know what had Gemma grinning ear to ear.

"Eee!" Gemma squealed and clapped her hands in excitement. "We're pregnant!"

Claire jerked back in surprise, her gaze flying to Jack's. He didn't look as ecstatic as his wife, but he did look happy, proud even.

A variety of emotions tumbled and twisted through her, and sadly, she couldn't deny that disappointment was one of them. Not that Gemma and Jack were having a baby; she refused to turn into a bitter ex-wife who begrudged them their happiness. It was the depressing confirmation that her ex could make a marriage work that selfishly bummed her out.

When Jack had filed for divorce, he'd made it painfully clear that she and their marriage had been a massive disappointment. He'd blamed the failure on her, saying she was too controlling and independent to be in any sort of lasting relationship. She'd always hoped he'd been wrong, attributing her failed marriage to their whirlwind romance, short engagement, and gap in age. But after the divorce, Jack had remarried the even younger Gemma, and Claire hadn't been on one single date that she actually enjoyed.

Maybe Jack had gotten it right. Maybe she had been the problem.

Shoving away her unease, Claire smiled widely. No matter what her issues, she'd never take it out on a baby or a pregnant woman. "That's wonderful news. Congratulations."

Gemma shot a victorious look at Jack still standing next to the table. "I told you Claire would be great." She wrinkled her nose in confusion at her husband. "Why are you still standing? Sit. Sit. Sit." She motioned for Jack to sit next to Ethan.

Ethan's brows shot up, and Jack grimaced. Looked like neither guy wanted to cozy up on the narrow booth bench.

Gemma grunted and rolled her eyes. "Boys are so silly." Laughing, she jumped to her feet, yanked Claire out of the booth, and shoved her down on the other side next to Ethan. "Here, you two sit together. Jack and I will sit across for you." In a flash of movement, she grabbed Jack's arm and pulled him into the booth with her. "OMG. Where are my manners?" She rolled her eyes again, then focused on Ethan. "I'm Gemma and this is Jack, and I know who you are, Ethan Dubois. I'm a really big fan!"

"Thanks, Gemma. It's always nice to meet a fan."

Gemma beamed. "How long have you two been going out?"

"Oh, no." Claire shook her head. "We aren't together." She elbowed Ethan. "Tell them we aren't together."

"Whatever you say, Boss." He dropped an arm around Claire's shoulders and turned to Gemma. "We aren't together," he said in the least convincing performance of all time.

"Why do you call her Boss?" Gemma asked, tilting her head in confusion.

Claire's stomach dropped. Hovering on the brink of mortification, she turned her head to meet his gaze, her eyes half pleading and half threatening to keep quiet about her earlier proposition.

"It's my pet name for her," Ethan said.

"She always was bossy," Jack grumbled under his breath.

Ethan's features hardened as he turned his attention to her ex. "Claire's a great leader. Only a weak man has a problem following a strong woman."

"That's so forward thinking of you." Gemma's eyes melted into pools of liquid chocolate as she placed her hand over her heart. "I love it!" she whisper-yelled with rushed enthusiasm. "You two have crazy, amazing chemistry."

"I'm trying to convince her of that very thing." Only a breath away, Ethan turned to lock a smoldering gaze on Claire while he kept his arm wrapped around her shoulders.

Claire didn't know if the hot, hungry look was for Gemma and Jack's benefit or if it was real. Either way, its intoxicating effect, combined with his defense of her, was making her head spin. She licked her dry lips and swallowed hard.

Ethan's eyes dropped to her mouth, and his arm tightened around her.

"Whoa," Gemma murmured. "Does Claire have a pet name for you?"

Ethan drew in a deep breath and tore his gaze away to look at Gemma. "Sorry, I lost my focus. It happens a lot when Claire's around. What did you ask me?"

Gemma's wide-eyed gaze darted between them. "I asked what she calls you."

A boyish grin split his face. "Lucky. She calls me Lucky, and I have to say"—he winked—"the name fits."

"OMG. Look at me." Gemma held up a hand. "I'm shaking from just watching you together."

"We're not together. We're just here to talk about soccer," Claire insisted to Gemma, Jack, Ethan, and maybe even herself.

"Soccer? Yeah, right." Gemma giggled. "Jack has never looked at me like that when we're talking about soccer." She clapped her hands again. "This is so awesome! You're dating Ethan DuBois! Tell me all about it!"

"Who's dating Ethan DuBois?" a familiar, very curious female voice asked from behind Claire.

She fought the groan building in her throat. Had she actually thought tonight would be easy? She should have realized Silver Bay was too small for her dinner with Ethan to go unnoticed.

"Hi, Kat." Claire sighed. "How long have you been lurking behind me?"

"I don't lurk. Even if I wanted to, I couldn't." The petite powerhouse stepped around to the end of their booth. "Big guy here"—Kat jerked her thumb at her tall, blond, built-like-Thor husband—"is too large to lurk."

"Hey, Logan." Claire greeted her brother-in-law with a grateful smile. He was her best chance at keeping Kat from saying anything too outrageous.

"Gotta admit," Kat said, eyeing the four of them in turn, "this is one frickin' bizarre-ass double date. Hi, Ethan. It's been a while."

Jack snorted. "It's hardly a double date. Gemma is saying hello to Claire, and now it's time for us to leave." He motioned for Gemma to get up.

"But I haven't met Kat's husband yet," she

protested.

"I'm sorry. How rude of me," Kat said, not sounding the least bit apologetic. She wrapped an arm around her husband's waist. "Logan, this is Gemma and Jackass."

They quickly exchanged greetings. Claire noted that Jack still looked ticked about the nickname Kat had insisted on calling him since the divorce. And how did Kat know Ethan?

"I've seen you play soccer," Logan said to Ethan. "You're good."

"Thanks. Australian?" Ethan asked, referring to Logan's accent.

"Yip," Logan confirmed, looking pleased to have his nationality recognized so quickly.

"I've played with a few Aussies in the past. Great guys. Lots of fun. Tough as hell."

"Sounds 'bout right. So how do you know Kat?"

Exactly what Claire wanted to know.

"We went to high school together." Ethan winked at Kat. "I used to have a major crush on her."

Kat laughed. "Seriously? You were so busy playing soccer I'm shocked you had time to notice me."

"It would've been harder *not* to notice you."

Ethan's expression and tone were light and playful. Even so, Claire felt an unexpected twinge of jealousy twist her belly. Judging by the low sound of warning emanating from the back of Logan's throat, he'd felt the same twinge.

Ethan's gaze shifted briefly to Logan, then back to Kat. "Congratulations on your marriage by the way. You two look very happy together."

"We have a son, too," Kat said. "Four months old."

"As fun as this trip down memory lane is, Gemma and I have to go," Jack drawled.

"Sounds good. Bye," Claire added, hoping to end this disastrous soccer date as soon as humanly possible.

"No way are we leaving now," Gemma said, shooting Jack a you're-totally-crazy look. "Claire is going to tell us more about her and Ethan." She turned back to Claire. "How long have you been going out?"

"They're not dating," Jack said to Gemma. "He's only in town short term. Everybody knows his retirement is a ploy for more money. He'll be gone before the end of the year. And even if a professional athlete was interested in Claire, she's too pragmatic to start dating someone who's leaving soon."

"Any man with a pulse would be interested in Claire," Ethan growled. "And my retirement isn't a ploy."

Gemma's brown eyes filled with sympathy. "I heard you're taking time off to get over your painful breakup with Quinn Knight."

"Who?" Jack, Kat, and Claire asked in unison.

Gemma rolled her eyes. "Am I the only one who reads *People* magazine? Quinn's a pop star who's touring right now to promote her new album, *Scandal*. Ethan was spotted pulling her panties out of his pocket."

Claire felt her eyebrows hit her hairline. "Sounds like an interesting story."

Ethan held up his hands in a gesture of

innocence. "Hey, I was just visiting an old teammate in LA. We were at the same club one night. She introduced herself and about five minutes into the conversation told me to check my pocket."

"Never mind." Claire threw her hand up to halt all progress. "I don't want to know the details."

"Somebody snapped a picture right when I pulled the frilly pink fabric from my shirt pocket like a frigging magician."

Kat snorted in laughter. "Come on, DuBois, you want us to believe you really didn't know her panties were in your pocket?"

"I had no idea. All I can figure is she slipped them in when she leaned forward to whisper in my ear. Trust me, I'm not into clingy, attention-seeking woman."

"I don't understand the logistics of that maneuver," Claire snapped. "How in the world did she get her panties off without anyone noticing?"

"The bathroom?" Ethan shrugged. "Or maybe she carries spares around in her purse to hand out like a calling card."

"Definitely makes an impression," Logan said, sounding a heck of a lot more amused by the story than Claire felt.

"Yeah, a trashy one," Kat said, elbowing Logan in the gut. "So," she purred, turning back to Claire, "Ethan DuBois is the young, unemployed stud you told us about. I guess that's what you meant when you said we'd understand when we saw him. Gotta admit, you surprised me. I didn't realize Ethan had been back in town that long. How'd you meet?"

In an instant, five sets of very curious eyes focused on Claire. She looked at Ethan. He stared back, appearing as interested in what she planned to say as everyone else. She raised her eyebrows in silent question. Ethan gave her a slight shrug and a crooked smile, silently saying he'd follow her lead.

Oh, what the hell. After her little announcement at lunch the other day and this disastrous soccer date, everyone would think they were going out anyway. She had a better chance of managing the situation if she took control now.

Feigning nonchalance, Claire leveled her little sis with a smug stare. "Ethan and I met in a bar a couple of weeks ago. We've seen each other a few times since then."

Amusement flashed in Kat's eyes. "In a bar? I'm impressed." She cocked an eyebrow. "So are you two dating?"

"Yes. I guess there's no hiding it now," Ethan said.

Claire could actually *feel* him smiling behind her. She resisted an eye roll and fought back a wave of unease, wondering again why he seemed so pleased to play the role of pretend boyfriend.

"Interesting." Kat's expression made it clear she knew darn well that would make Claire ineligible for the auction.

"Just to be safe, you should probably move me to a different role in your fundraiser," Claire offered helpfully.

"Nice try, sis, but we'll keep you on the list for now. A lot could change between now and October."

"What list?" Gemma piped in, looking oblivious to the veiled battle between sisters.

"Claire's offered to take part in the bachelor and

bachelorette auction I've organized for the charity I run, SAS, in mid-October." Kat turned her attention to Ethan. "You'd be a valuable addition to our lineup. What chance do I have of talking you into offering your services for the evening?"

"Not gonna happen." Ethan shook his head. "I did one of those a few years back. It didn't end well. But I'm happy to donate whatever amount you think a date with me would sell for."

Kat's eyes lit with approval. "Excellent. That should fund our operation for at least a month."

"Happy to help," Ethan replied.

"Wait. What?" Claire gasped. "You didn't tell me I could buy my way out."

"You can't. That golden-girl reputation of yours is priceless when it comes to locking in other volunteers. There's only one path that leads out of this auction for you. But I think you've already figured that out, haven't ya?" Kat winked and clicked her tongue.

"All right, tiger. Let's go home. You've caused enough ruckus for one evening." Logan slid his hand to Kat's lower back.

"Really?" Kat asked, eyeing Logan up and down. "I can think of a few more ways to cause a ruckus before the night is over."

"Even more reason to get you home," he murmured to his wife. "Cheers," he said as way of goodbye to the rest of them and hustled Kat toward the door.

"We're going too." Jack sounded annoyed. "Or would you rather spend the entire evening with my ex-wife?"

"Fine," Gemma relented with an eye roll, sliding

from the booth. "Bye, Claire. And it was really nice meeting you, Ethan." She tossed the words over her shoulder as Jack steered her away.

Claire watched their hasty departure. Hoping to delay the inevitable, she continued to stare at the door after they'd gone. She felt Ethan's eyes on her. She sensed his curiosity and his amusement. He must have a hundred questions.

She didn't want to answer any of them.

For the second time that evening, Claire felt the uncharacteristic desire to make a run for it. Assuming Ethan even tried to catch her, she might be able to beat him to the door. She'd always been fast, and mortification gave her an edge. But his long, muscled legs and athletic, agile body played in his favor. When she threw her heels and skinny jeans into the equation, she started to feel like the gazelle in one of those morbid wildlife shows.

Resigned to her fate, she blew out a hefty sigh and cocked her head toward his. "Any chance we can act like the last fifteen minutes never happened?"

"Nope." He grinned. "Looks like I'm your boyfriend for the next couple of months."

She ground her teeth and resisted rolling her eyes at her own idiocy. "Fine. I accept your offer to help me. Let's wait a couple of weeks and go to a movie."

"That's too long of a wait and too private a setting to work. We should make it clear we're dating at the team pool party at my house next Saturday."

"One of the moms dating the hot, young coach?" Her voice cracked with strain. "That's sure to get Silver Bay talking." She cringed.

"It'll be fun. Trust me." His Cheshire cat grin didn't inspire much trust.

"Parents on the team might complain that Ty will get special treatment if we're dating. It could cause problems for you."

"I can handle the parents on the team," Ethan said.

"What about your mom?" Claire asked, curious to see his reaction. "Will she be at the pool party? You mentioned it's her house."

His jaw tensed. "*New* house. A gift from me she hasn't quite warmed up to yet."

"Translation—your mom refuses to move into the house you bought for her." She feigned an innocent expression. "Or have I misunderstood what's going on between you two?"

Frustration marred his features. "The house is great. Everything she could ever want." He shook his head. "Maybe it needs to be painted or something."

Claire eyed him skeptically. Odds were good whatever issue Ethan's mom had with the house went deeper than the color of the walls. "Why don't you invite her to the party?"

He went brows up. "You want to meet my mother?"

"You're helping me. I'll help you," Claire offered, jumping at the chance to balance out the power structure between them. "I'll see if I can figure out what her concerns are about the house."

"Okay. I'll ask her." He shrugged and took a drink from his beer. "Mom loves kids, so having the team there might actually get her through the front door."

"Wait. What?" Claire gave her head a quick shake, assuming she'd missed something. "Your mom has never been inside the house you bought for her?"

"She can be ... stubborn." He more sighed than said the words, his disheartened tone tugging at Claire's heart.

She gently bumped his shoulder with hers. "Buck up, Lucky. I'm good at fixing problems. Maybe I can help with yours."

SEVEN

"THERE'S someone here to see you. Want me to get rid of him?"

Claire looked up from her computer. Martha Gibbs, her father's executive assistant, stood in her doorway, alert and ready to defend. With her ample bosom and a sturdy German frame, Martha could snap interlopers like a twig.

It was Wednesday afternoon and Claire had been studying numbers for the last hour. Her mind felt like a heap of mathematical mush. "That's okay. I can see him now. I could use a break from spreadsheets." She closed her laptop and reached her hands over her head to stretch her cramped muscles.

"Okay," Martha said with sharp interest in her perceptive brown eyes. "I'll send him back."

Martha had been at Bennett Industries since graduating from community college twenty-five years ago. Her work ethic—learned from growing up on a dairy farm—had set her apart and launched her to the position of Mr. Bennett's executive assistant within five years. She was smart, efficient, and intimidating. Claire liked her a lot.

Claire glanced at her watch, slipped on her heels, and rose from her desk. She'd told Bernie from

Human Resources to stop by her office at the end of the day to discuss a compensation issue they were having with a new employee. He must have decided to swing by early.

In need of caffeine, she moved to the elaborate wet bar along the office wall and leaned over to retrieve the pitcher of iced tea from the refrigerator.

Strong, confident footsteps strode down the hall and stopped at her open office door. As Claire straightened, the air pressure shifted and her nipples tightened. Even with her back to the door, she knew her visitor definitely was not Bernie from Human Resources. Not only did Bernie shuffle wherever he went, he lacked the ability to affect a barometer or her nipples.

"Corner office. I'm impressed."

Every sensitive nerve on the back of her neck came alive at the sound of the deep timbre in Ethan's voice. She closed her eyes, inhaled slowly, and fought the urge to squirm as awareness coursed through her. Opening her eyes, she poured a glass of tea and turned to face him.

"It's my dad's office, not mine" she said. "I work in here when he's out since it's better equipped for meetings." She gestured toward both the wet bar and the large conference table on the opposite side of the room.

"How often is he out of the office?"

"Depends on the week." Her vague reply came more from habit than from the desire to keep her dad's frequent absenteeism a secret from Ethan.

For the past few years, Richard Bennett had made a show of coming to the office every morning at nine. He had a cup of coffee, chatted with his favorite employees, got an update from Claire on any important matters, and hit the road most days by ten o'clock. He did check emails throughout the day, and promptly forwarded them to her to handle.

"So where's your office?" Ethan raised an eyebrow in question.

"Oh. Well, I guess I don't technically have one." Claire tucked her hair behind one ear. "No matter. This one is big enough for both of us."

Ethan scanned the large room, taking in the conference table, the oversized walnut desk for one-on-one meetings, and sitting area with a love seat and two armchairs for casual conversations.

He turned back to her, good-natured humor in his eyes. "It's nice you two can manage in such a tight space."

"It's a real hardship." She gestured towards the casual sitting area. "Can I get you a drink?"

"I'll have whatever you're having." Ethan nodded to her glass before taking a seat in one of the armchairs by the wet bar.

"You got it." She poured another iced tea, handed it to him, and sat down on the love seat, trying to ignore the fact that her legs were only inches from his. "I talked to Ty about the ODP program if that's why you stopped by. He wants to go for it, so I registered him for tryouts. Thanks for suggesting it. He's really excited."

"Happy to help," Ethan said, sniffing his drink with a dubious expression on his too-handsome face.

"Iced tea," she said with a laugh. "Not scotch."

He grinned at her. "Damn. The idea of you trying to get me drunk has its merits."

She rolled her eyes and bit back a grin. "Was

there anything else you wanted, Ethan?"

His gaze darkened and he tipped his head to study her with a smoldering expression.

"Well," she amended, setting her drink on the table next to her, "besides *that*."

He chuckled, amusement effectively replacing his smolder. "What kind of boyfriend would I be if I didn't visit you at work?"

"The pretend kind."

"I always aim to over-deliver no matter what position I'm playing. It works well for me."

"So this visit is an example of you over-delivering?"

"Absolutely. I figured we should decide on a strategy for the pool party on Saturday. I think you should arrive early. We'll look more coupley if you're there to greet everyone with me."

Claire arch a brow. "Coupley?"

"Yeah." His lips turned up in an undeterred smile. "It'll send a nonverbal message that we're together. Trust me."

"Okay." She shrugged, amused and a little impressed by his dedication to the ruse. "We'll get there early."

"I should also warn you that my mom accepted my offer and will be there too."

"Warn me? Interesting choice of words."

His humor faded. "Mom has strong opinions and sees no reason to keep them to herself which at time makes her ..." He paused, considering his next words. "Argumentative."

"No worries. You've met Kat. I can handle argumentative."

"Mom makes Kat look like a kitten. Don't tell

Kat I said that," he hurried to add.

"Afraid of Logan?"

"Hell, no. I'm afraid of Kat." Ethan took a sip of his iced tea and frowned. "I've never gotten used to leaf-flavored water. Mom loves the stuff. Says it's better for you than all those sugar-infested sports drinks. You can imagine her reaction to seeing me in a Gatorade commercial," he added dryly.

"Ty showed me that one last night. I liked it." Claire managed to hold her voice impressively neutral considering the enormity of that understatement. Watching the commercialized version of the gorgeous man in front of her racing down a field, his muscled body skillfully evading everyone in his path as he maneuvered the ball with a combination of grace and power, had kicked both her pulse and her guilt into overdrive. Her son had been trying to show off his coach's awesome footwork, and Ethan's feet were the only part of his body she *hadn't* been watching while the video played.

"I'm glad someone did. Mom definitely did not enjoy it." He sat back in the chair and blew out an exaggerated breath. "She blasted me on the phone for an hour after it aired. Compared it to selling crack at a playground."

Claire winced. "An extreme comparison."

"She has a few hot buttons. That's another reason why I stopped by. When you meet her Saturday, it's best if you don't bring up my father. That topic always sets her off."

Now she was the one to choose her words carefully. "Care to share the details?"

He studied her for a moment, his bright-blue

eyes flashing with a mixture of emotions. "Like I said the other night, mom loves kids. She didn't feel the need to be in a relationship before having one."

"Sperm donor?"

His brows arched in surprise. "Yeah. You don't look surprised. People usually assume my dad left us. Which always ticks her off."

"She sounds like a strong woman, and it would take a lot of strength to make that decision," Claire said. "Also, there's no mention of your father online."

"You looked me up?" Ethan asked, sounding pleased she'd taken the time to research him.

"Don't read too much into it. It simply seemed the most efficient way to learn more about you."

"Find out anything interesting?"

"Lots. You started playing professional soccer at eighteen. On the national team, you started in two different World Cups. In Major League Soccer, you played five years in LA and then six years in Chicago and signed a major endorsement deal with Nike. During the eleven years you played in the MLS, you scored 133 goals and were making a run at becoming the highest goal scorer in MLS history before you unexpectedly retired at the end of last season." She stopped recounting his impressive stats to draw in a breath. "Of course, most people believe your retirement isn't permanent and that you're using it as a negotiation strategy to force Chicago to up your salary. The consensus is you'll be back on the field at the start of next season—if not sooner."

"I'm retired."

"Currently," she said, matching the curtness in his voice. "I talked to my kids about you. I told them we met before you started coaching Ty's team and that I like spending time with you. I let them know we are going on a few dates while you're in Silver Bay. But I made it very clear it's unlikely you'll be in town for long."

"Why do you assume I won't be in town long?"

"You don't have a long-term job or home of your own, and as far as I can see, you have no intention of getting either one of them here. And you've only committed to coaching the boys through the season's end in November." She rested her elbow on the arm of the love seat and crossed her legs, confident in her assessment. "My instincts tell me you're in Silver Bay to take care of a few things— most likely concerning your mother and the house you bought her—while you work stuff out with your old team or a new team or whatever it is that you're planning for your future."

Ethan took another sip of tea and grimaced, obviously forgetting the contents of the glass. He glared at the offending liquid. "Maybe I haven't got anything planned for my future," he said, his voice tight.

She shrugged. "It's possible. But I'd be surprised if a successful pro-athlete retired young and in good health solely to live off endorsement deals for the rest of his days."

Ethan drew in a long breath, leaned forward, and propped his elbows on his knees. "You're incredibly perceptive," he said, absently swirling the glass of tea in his hand as if it really were a scotch. "It's a little intimidating."

Tension straightened her spine. Jack used to complain that people found her intimidating, saying they couldn't relax around her. "Sorry." She didn't mean to stress people out. She honestly didn't know what she did that was so intimidating. "I don't know how to stop."

"Why would you want to stop? It's damn sexy," he drawled with a wicked, dimpled grin.

The grin promised trouble ... or pleasure ... or both.

Her nipples tightened again. *Sheesh*. What was wrong with her? She usually had control in spades.

Claire cleared her throat and pulled her wayward thoughts back on track. "You find intimidation sexy?" she asked, aiming to put him on the defensive for once. "That's borderline disturbing."

Looking more amused than offended, Ethan sat back, propped an ankle on one knee, and stationed his laced fingers behind his head in a relaxed position of confidence. "I like to be challenged," he said unapologetically. "I never enjoyed an easy win in soccer. My favorite games were the close, adrenaline-pumping matches against skilled opponents that I both feared and respected. It's a major rush to know if you lose focus for even a second, you're going down."

Clarity blazed through her. "That's it!" Claire sprang from the love seat. "That's why you're doing this. You're a world-class competitor, and you can't resist the challenge of wooing a woman who doesn't want to be wooed."

"That's not entirely true," he said in a soothing voice as he slowly rose from the chair.

"But it's not entirely untrue either. Right?"

He blasted her with his dimpled, brighter-than-the-sun smile. "You send off a vibe that you're happy with yourself and happy with your life without a guy in it. It's a rare trait. Any guy ... hell, every guy would be drawn to it."

"At least I understand your motivation now," she grumbled, pacing to the large wall of windows and blindly staring out.

"There are a lot of reasons why I'm attracted to you, Claire. You're beautiful, intelligent, funny, and capable. And yes, I also like the fact that you challenge me."

She turned back to face him. "I've got a busy life, a full life. I'm not playing hard to get or whatever you think I'm doing. I don't have the time or desire"—*or maybe even the ability*—"to manage a relationship."

He nodded his head in agreement. "I understand."

"Oh." Surprised he'd given up so quickly, her voice dropped an octave halfway through the word. "Good. I'm, um, glad."

She was glad he'd given up on her, right? Why wouldn't she be? The sinking feeling of disappointment in her belly couldn't be about Ethan.

"Yeah, I understand completely," Ethan drawled as he walked toward her, stopping a foot away. "You had a bad experience and now you need convincing that playing on a team is better than playing solo. And as a former professional athlete of a team-based sport, I'm the perfect guy to convince you." Ethan leaned down and brushed a kiss on her cheek. "See you Saturday, Boss."

EIGHT

SATURDAY afternoon, Claire pulled her SUV to a stop in front of a gorgeous two-story lakefront home that matched the address Ethan had given her. The cottage-style house had gray shake siding, white trim, a plethora of windows, and an oversized back deck she could see from the driveway.

With no neighboring homes in sight, Ethan's place sat on a huge lot with lots of shade trees and a private beach. While large and obviously new, the house somehow managed to maintain its charm, something most high-end construction failed to do.

She cut the engine and turned to look at her kiddos in the backseat. "This must be it. Make sure you take your swim bags."

"Lit!" Ty grabbed his bag and hopped from the car. Giddy with excitement, he bolted toward the backyard where Ethan had instructed the team to head upon arrival.

"I wish you would've worn the dress I picked out for you," Grace grumbled, absently toying with a strand of her long blond hair. "You look so pretty in it."

And here we go again, Claire thought, eyeing her petite nine-year-old with a mixture of exasperation, amusement, and love. "I like what I'm wearing." She gestured to her simple white maxi dress with a red band around her waist. "Besides, it's Labor Day weekend. I wanted to be patriotic."

"You looked like a princess in my dress."

"You watch too many Disney movies," Claire teased, climbing from the car and opening the back door.

"Grandma said you loved princess stories when you were a kid," Grace countered.

"I did," she conceded. "And I know you're trying to help, which is really cool of you. But I told you, sunshine, Ethan is only in Silver Bay for a few months. That's not enough time for anything lasting to develop between two people. Please don't get your hopes up."

"Dad said he fell in love with Gemma the moment he saw her."

He used to say the same thing about me, Claire thought, resisting an eye roll. In hindsight, she should have realized her relationship with Jack had been built on little more than physical attraction and short-lived romantic euphoria. If they had dated longer before rushing into marriage, they would've likely figured that out. Once the bright rays of reality had burned off the foggy haze of romance, they learned too late that they weren't compatible.

"Your dad and Gemma are lucky to have found each other," Claire replied, shooting for a diplomatic tone. "Now let's focus on the pool party instead of my dating life." She extended her hand to Grace. "It's so pretty and sunny. We don't have many more days of swimming left this summer, so we better enjoy it."

"Fine," Grace murmured, climbing out of the car after dramatically heaving the bag onto her shoulder as if it were full of books rather than a swim towel, goggles, and a change of pint-sized clothes.

Fighting a smile, Claire hugged Grace to her side and dropped a kiss on top of her head. As always, love squeezed her heart at the feel of her daughter's silky strands and the fresh scent of strawberry shampoo. "Love you, kiddo," she said to Grace before retrieving a large veggie tray from the backseat and bumping the door shut with her hip.

"Love you too," Grace said, falling in step beside Claire as they followed Ty's route to the backyard.

Claire had worried telling her kids about Ethan would upset them. Her stomach had been in knots the entire day leading up to her big announcement. A totally wasted day of worry considering after she told them, they'd bounced around the house cheering like she'd just scored the winning goal in a big game. Ty's reaction hadn't surprised her. Ethan walked on water in her son's opinion. Grace's better-than-going-to-Disneyworld excitement, however, had thrown her for a loop.

She still hadn't figured out if Grace liked the idea of her dating Ethan or if she just liked the idea of her dating *anyone*. From her build, to her features, to her temperament, Grace resembled Claire as a kid in a ton of ways. Odds were good Grace might have also inherited Claire's past delusional fantasies that blurred romance and love. She'd need to gently and repeatedly remind Grace that it was okay for two people to go on a few dates and then go their separate ways. Romance did not always equal love.

When they rounded the rear corner of the house,

Claire's step faltered. "Holy smokes."

The backyard looked more like a five-star resort than a private residence. A massive stone and wood deck spanned the middle level of the house. Below that, a wall of glass windows and a sliding door led into a walkout basement. A flight of stairs from the deck landed on a brick paver patio featuring a lagoon-style pool with a rock grotto and waterfall at the far end. Farther on, the yard slopped gently downward before leading to a sandy beach, then eventually the lake about fifty yards away.

"Whoa," Grace murmured beside her, sounding as stunned as Claire felt.

Claire had assumed the house would be nice. She hadn't known it would leave nice coughing and sputtering in its dust.

"Hi, ladies," Ethan called from the edge of the pool. "Ty challenged me to a cannonball competition. Winner gets bragging rights. Care to enter the contest?"

"That pool is massively cool," Claire said to Grace. "What do you say, sunshine? Are you going to let them have all the fun?"

Grace looked up at Claire, her perfect, heart-shaped face beaming with excitement. "Heck no. I'm going to win." She grinned. "Wait for me!" Grace yelled, racing toward the pool.

Love swelled Claire's heart as she watched her little girl peel away her cover-up and kick off her flip-flops on her mad dash to the pool. She couldn't believe how much her kids had aged in the last year. Before she knew it, they'd be in college and she'd be … Claire gave her head a quick shake, not wanting to finish the thought.

"Are you the beautiful mother of two I'm supposed to meet?"

Startled, Claire whipped around to find a tall, stern-looking woman standing directly behind her. Judging by the amount of gray in her chin-length bob and the lines around her bright blue eyes, Claire placed her somewhere in her fifties. This must be Ethan's mom.

She smiled, shifted the veggie tray to her left arm and extended her right hand. "I'm Claire Bennett."

"Maxine DuBois. Ethan's mother," she confirmed, shaking Claire's hand with a firm grip. "Don't take this the wrong way, but I believe my son might be using you."

"Is there a right way to take that?" Claire asked, hiding her surprise with an even tone. Her father had taught her the importance of keeping a clear head and an open mind. Emotions could screw up any business deal, especially an unorthodox deal like the one she had with Ethan.

"As bait. To get me to this house. My son is using you as bait. Ethan has a rather extraordinary IQ. I'm sure it was quite simple for him to realize I wouldn't be able to resist meeting a girlfriend, especially one with two children."

Huh? Claire couldn't tell if she'd just been insulted. It certainly felt like she had, but Maxine's clipped, cool tone would likely make any statement sound like an insult. "Well, whatever the reason, I'm glad you decided to join the party."

"How did you meet my son?"

"Ethan is my son Ty's soccer coach."

Maxine pressed her lips so tightly together they paled from loss of blood flow. "Yes." She wrinkled her nose in distaste. "Ethan told me about his new ... job."

"You don't care for Ethan's career choice?"

"Soccer isn't a career. It's a sport."

"In this country alone, professional soccer generates around a half a billion dollars in revenue a year." Claire silently thanked Wikipedia for providing that nugget of knowledge during her online research to find out more about Ethan.

"That simply proves Americans are willing to spend a ridiculous amount of money on a game."

Yikes. She'd just met Ethan's mom, and she'd already hit a hot button. Time to lighten the mood. "What's your opinion on cannonball competitions? Care to participate?" Claire asked, motioning at the pool with an innocent expression.

"Regrettably, I didn't bring swimwear," Maxine said, not sounding the least bit regretful.

"Then you can be the judge." Claire started down the steps artistically built into the landscape. "Come on, or they'll start without us."

Even though Maxine hesitated behind her, Claire felt sure she would eventually join them. Ethan said his mother was argumentative, and argumentative people didn't usually run away. Instead, they tended to stick around and ... well, argue.

Near the edge of the pool, Claire plopped her beach bag on a navy-and-white striped cushioned chaise, shaded her eyes with one hand, and looked to the jumpers standing atop the five-foot waterfall. "Who's up first?"

"Me!" Grace yelled, jumping in with a loud squeal. She hit the water with an impressive splash for a fifty-pound lightweight.

As soon as she cleared the area, Ty leaped off. His size advantage carried him farther and higher than his sister, but he didn't stay in as tight of a ball.

His head popped above the water. "How'd I do?" he asked, wiping water from his eyes.

"Great! But Ethan still has to go, and he's a world-class competitor."

"True," Ethan confirmed with a mischievous smile. "And I always play to win."

Claire bit back a grin and rolled her eyes. "Just jump, Lucky, or I'll give you a yellow card for stalling."

"You bet, Boss." He winked and stepped off the edge, his fully grown, fully muscled body launching a massive wave on impact.

"Phew," Claire said as soon as all three heads were above water. "Glad I'm not the judge."

"Who is?" Ty asked, looking around.

"Ethan's mom," Claire told them, glancing over her shoulder.

Maxine stood halfway between the pool and the steps leading to the driveway. Even though her expression resembled a disapproving school marm, her body language betrayed nerves. Not only did she clutch her purse tightly to her body, she also shifted her weight from foot to foot as if not quite sure where she should stand.

Claire would hate to be that uncomfortable around one of her own kids. Empathy tugged at her heart, increasing her desire to help fix whatever had caused the rift between Ethan and his mom.

She gave Maxine an encouraging smile and extended her arm in a come-on-over-and-join-me gesture. "Maxine, I'd like to introduce you to my kiddos." She paused, waiting for Ethan's mom to move closer.

Maxine stared at her a moment and gave a slight nod. "Yes. That's why I'm here," she said almost to herself.

As Maxine approached, Grace, Ty, and Ethan climbed from the pool. Claire tossed them towels, waited for his mom to reach them, and made brief introductions.

"You both had excellent jumps into the pool," Maxine said, a smile with unexpected warmth replacing her reserved expression. "At this point, it's really too close to call. Would you be willing to jump a few more times so I can calculate a cumulative score to decide the winner?"

"Sure," Ty answered, nodding his head in enthusiasm.

"What about Ethan? Are you going to ask him to jump again?" Grace asked, looking over her shoulder to where Ethan stood a few feet away.

Maxine shifted her gaze to her son, the smile slipping from her lips. "No. Ethan does whatever he wants."

Ouch. Claire saw Ethan tense. He waited for the kids to head toward the pool's waterfall before moving to stand next to Claire.

"Hi, Mom. Thanks for joining us."

"As long as your intentions are truly to introduce me to Claire and those two adorable children, I'm happy to be here. If, however, this is an ill-advised attempt to convince me to move into this oversized home, then I'm afraid you're wasting your time."

"I bought this house for you," Ethan said, his tone a mixture of frustration and annoyance. "If you'd only give it a chance, you'd see that it's perfect."

"Not for me." Maxine shook her head and compressed her lips so tightly they started to turn white again.

"This is the type of home we always dreamed of moving into when I was a kid," Ethan argued. "Now I can afford to give that to you."

Maxine's eyes flared. "I could have afforded a big house when you were a child, Ethan. But I chose then—and I choose now—to spend my money and my time wisely. I've no desire to take care of such a large property. Look at this place." She gestured to the estate with a dramatic sweep of her hand. "It's not designed for a single occupant. Besides, I like my home. It fits me and is close to the university."

Ethan closed his eyes and squeezed the bridge of his nose. "I didn't expect you to pay for the maintenance. I'll hire a crew to take care of everything for you."

"You're not listening to me," Maxine snapped.

"I always listen," Ethan sighed, opening his eyes.

"You most certainly do not listen to me." Maxine's expression looked chilly enough to freeze the pool. She clutched her purse in front of her body. "I think it's best if I—"

"Oh look," Claire interrupted. "The kids are waiting for you to watch them jump again, Maxine. Sit down and enjoy the cannonball show. Ethan and I need to get things ready in the kitchen before the rest of the team arrives."

"Kids," Claire yelled to Ty and Grace. "Ethan's mom is going to lifeguard while we go inside to set up for the party." She pushed Ethan gently toward the house. "We'll be right back. Yell if you need us."

"Time to regroup," she whispered, following him up a stairway leading to the expansive deck.

"Did I mention she can be argumentative?" Ethan sounded exasperated as he stepped through the glass door separating the deck from the kitchen. "Look at this place. I bought her the best of everything." He stabbed a finger toward a high-end gas range. "The range and hood alone cost more than a lot of new cars. The fridge was nearly as much, and the cabinets—"

"Are from Bennett Industries premier line which is custom made by our finest craftsmen and likely cost more than all of the appliances combined," Claire finished, sliding the door closed to stop their voices from carrying.

Ethan turned to her with a sheepish smile. "Sorry. Forgot who I was talking to."

"No need to apologize. Parents can be frustrating sometimes."

"It's been like this for years." He began kneading the back of his neck.

"When's the last time you two spent time together for fun?"

"You met her. She's not exactly a 'fun' kinda mom."

"Okay. Maybe fun was the wrong word. When's the last time you were together without debating your opposing opinions?"

Ethan opened his mouth to answer, then froze, a frown creasing his brow. "Years," he said on a drawn-out sigh. "It started back in high school. She wanted me to focus on academics, not soccer. She lost it when I decided to skip college to play professionally."

"Most parents would have been proud."

"Mom teaches mathematics at the university. She's devoted her life to academics and can't understand why I chose a sport over a degree. I come home at least once a year to see her, and we always end up fighting."

"Let's break that pattern." Claire gave him an encouraging smile. "For the rest of the afternoon and evening, we'll avoid all argument-inducing topics."

Ethan cocked a skeptical eyebrow. "Not sure that's possible."

"Sure, it is." She chucked him on the shoulder. "Once all the families from the team arrive, you'll have to play host. That will give you a good reason to step away if you feel an argument brewing. I'll help by changing the subject anytime I sense tension."

He gave a humorless chuckle. "You're going to be changing the subject a lot."

"So? I don't care if your mom thinks I have an attention problem as long as it lets you two spend some quality time together." She stepped closer and placed her hand on his arm.

She felt him tense beneath her touch and snatched her hand back. "Sorry."

"Don't be." He reached out and linked his fingers through hers. He slowly raised her hand to his lips and brushed a light kiss on her heated skin. "I liked it," he murmured, his low voice rumbling against her sensitive nerves.

So did she. Too much. "Ethan ..." Her whisper trailed off, making it obvious she had no flipping clue what to say next.

"Claire," he answered in a sexy timbre. Lowering their joined hands, he stepped closer until their bodies were only inches apart.

She tipped her head back to look up at him. She could feel the heat from his body and smell the mixture of chlorine and the summer sun rising from his skin. Only their hands touched, but her body purred in awareness.

"Unless you stop me in the next few seconds, I'm going to kiss you," he murmured lowering his head toward hers.

She should step away. She should remind both of them this relationship was a farce, nothing more than a solution to a problem. She should do a lot of responsible things. For once in her life, she didn't do any of them.

Claire gripped his hand tighter, lifted to her tiptoes, and pressed her lips to Ethan's, meeting and matching his kiss. He moaned a husky sigh in response and set about slowly, thoroughly exploring her lips with his. The sweet kiss went on for countless moments. Neither tried to deepen it—both content to keep it soft, gentle, and romantic.

Romantic? The word blazed through Claire's brain like a flashing sign warning of danger ahead. She'd learned romance was nothing more than a quickly fading illusion. After her failed marriage, she thought she'd killed her romantic tendencies, yanking the nasty weed from her heart. Now, with the slightest bit of nourishment, it had reared its ugly head.

She scrambled backwards. "Ethan, I—"

"We've got company," he quietly interrupted, his gaze shifting to something behind her.

Company? Her stomach sank to the polished wooden floor as she wondered exactly who had caught them locking lips.

With a mental cringe, Claire did a slow one-eighty to discover about half the team's parents and players standing on the deck outside of the kitchen, the wide wall of windows providing no visual division between the two spaces. Some parents were jockeying for a better position. Some were covering their kid's eyes. All of them were wearing the same stunned expression.

"Smile," Ethan said, throwing his arm over her shoulder. "It's game time."

NINE

IN her professional life, Claire handled stressful situations with a combination of clear-headed thinking and trust-inspiring composure. Known for her cool confidence, people from all over the company came to her when issues spiraled out of control. Claire had a way of breaking even the biggest crises down into manageable pieces.

She'd like to think she faced stressors in her personal life with the same aplomb. If the way she remained rooted to the kitchen floor, staring saucer-eyed and open-mouthed was anything to go by, then she seriously sucked at dealing with crises in her personal life.

"Breathe," Ethan soothed, likely in response to the nervous, slightly bizarre, guttural sound coming from the back of her throat.

He kept a casual arm around her shoulders, guided her forward, and slid the door open. "Welcome, guys. Make yourself at home. Hop in the pool, check out the beach, or grab a drink and enjoy the patio." He sounded completely comfortable with her inches from his side. "We were just about to fire up the grill."

Needing no further invitation, the kids bolted

from the deck in a rush of excited chatter. A few seconds later, splashes from bodies hitting the water and laughter filled the air.

The team's parents weren't so easily distracted.

"So, you two are … ?" Chuck Lenley, the town's best electrician and dad of the team's top defender, gestured between Claire and Ethan with a tentative, curious expression on his lean face.

"Together," Ethan filled in the blank.

Heather Haventale shouldered her way to the front. "Isn't that a major conflict of interest? My son shouldn't sit the bench because she's"—Heather curled her lip and pointed at Claire—"working it." She crossed her arms and glared, outrage oozing from her short frame.

Claire ground her teeth to stop herself from telling Heather to shut the hell up. From the amount of time her son played in a game to the team's uniform color, the woman whined about everything. She was one of those utterly annoying people who failed to understand the compromises and trust required from being on a team.

"Every decision I make regarding the team is based on what I think is best for the boys' development as soccer players, teammates, and— more importantly to me—decent human beings." Like any great leader, Ethan's voice carried an authoritative weight that managed to inspire confidence and head off dissent. "But I'm the new guy here," he said with a charming smile, his tone going light and friendly. "I can ask to be transferred to a different team if you all don't feel comfortable that I'm dating Claire."

Well played, Claire thought, biting back a smile as

an overwhelming chorus of support for Ethan to remain coach thundered through the air. Shaking her head like crazy, even Heather looked panicked at the thought, likely not wanting to be known as the woman who drove a world-class coach from the team's roster.

"Okay," Ethan said, beaming at his adoring fans with an aw-shucks expression. "It's settled. I'll coach the team and date this beautiful lady." He pulled her close to his side and dropped a playful kiss on top of her head. "I'm a lucky guy," he murmured next to her ear.

She rolled her eyes and elbowed him in the gut. But truthfully, her elbow lacked any real force and lingered—of its own accord, she was pretty sure—against his muscled abs a little longer than necessary. She knew his adoration was an exaggerated act for the audience. Honestly, she did. But that didn't stop her heart from doing flip-flops every time he flirted with her, or touched her, or murmured *anything* next to her ear.

Thankfully, the rest of the evening passed by quickly in a festive blur of activity. Claire bounced between feeding hungry kids, sidestepping questions about her love life, and eavesdropping on conversations between Ethan and his mom in case things started to escalate.

She could tell Ethan was doing his best to keep the peace, and it looked like his mom wanted to get along as well, even if she did sneak in a few zingers. At one point or another, Claire heard her complain about Ethan's career choice, his lack of a college degree, and, of course, his "nonsensical housing purchase."

Each time, Claire made up an excuse to pull Ethan away before old battles could flare back to life. By the time the last two families packed up their soggy swim bags and headed for home around nine o'clock, she could see the signs of stress building around Ethan's eyes.

"You did good tonight," Claire said, helping Ethan pull inflatable toys from the pool.

Still in his board shorts, he tossed a grin over his shoulder as he snatched the lanky neck of a giant blow-up flamingo and hauled it from its watery home. "Thanks. I knew the team's parents would see things my way. I wish I could say the same thing about my mom." He deposited the flamingo on the pool deck to dry and looked around. "Did she leave?"

"Nope," Claire said, picking up balls and dive sticks scattered around the pool. "I told Ty and Grace to take her around the house on a self-guided tour while we cleaned up out here."

"Great idea." He eyed her with an impressed look as he walked closer. "Maybe she'll be more positive about it if I'm not the one showing her around."

"That's my hope. Plus, I wanted to discuss our next date without an audience. Would next Saturday night work for dinner and a movie?"

"I might have plans for next Saturday. How about Friday night instead?"

"Plans?" Hurt and surprise slashed through her. "Are you two-timing your pretend girlfriend with a real one, Lucky?"

"I'm trying to." He grinned.

She narrowed her eyes and poked him hard in

the chest. "You're the one who insisted on helping."

He cocked his head. "Even though you're absolutely adorable right now, there's no need to be jealous. I—"

"I'm not jealous," she snapped. "I have no right to be jealous. We aren't together. The idea of you with another woman doesn't bother me at all. I don't even care who she is." Claire crossed her arms and glared, unable to stop her foot from tapping impatiently atop the brick patio pavers. "Solely out of curiosity, who is she?"

"You."

Her foot stopped tapping. "Me?"

"Yeah. I called in a favor and have four tickets to the soccer match in Chicago on Saturday. I want to take you and the kids." He shrugged. "Grace mentioned she doesn't enjoy soccer as much, so I thought we could hit the zoo in the afternoon before the match for her."

Claire swallowed hard, inexplicably touched he'd not only included her kids, but he'd planned a day based on what they'd like to do. "That sounds really nice. They'll love it. We can skip plans for Friday night and make Saturday our weekly date instead."

"If you want people to believe you're gaga over me, it's okay if we see each other more than once a week."

She drew in a breath and opened her mouth, ready to argue.

"Nope." He shook his head. "Soccer practice doesn't count."

She went brows up. "How do you read me so easily?" She shot up her hand in a stop-right-there gesture. "Never mind. I don't want to know."

Turning from him, Claire picked up her beach bag and started gathering her kids' clothes, goggles, and towels.

"You know I'm right."

Avoiding eye contact, she crammed a dripping towel into the flowery bag. "Fine. We don't have to always limit our dates to once a week. We do need to remember that our pretend relationship ends mid-October."

"Absolutely." He winked.

Claire dropped a pair of goggles into the bag and eyed him suspiciously. "I get nervous when you're this agreeable."

"I'm always agreeable," he countered.

She hefted the bag to her shoulder, then shifted it in front of her—using it like some sort of overstuffed, soggy, floral shield against him. "Good. Then we both agree this only lasts until the auction."

"Whatever you say. Now we should finish cleaning up before Mom breaks into her lecture on why students need to take as much math as possible." Ethan scooped a thick foam mat from the water with ease, his wet body glistening in the landscape lighting. "While it's a real crowd pleaser with her mathematics buddies, Grace and Ty will never want to hang with us again if they have to smile and nod through the unabridged version."

Claire tore her gaze from Ethan's bare torso as he walked by with the mat and cleared her throat. "Um. Yeah. Okay," she mumbled, scanning the area for a distraction. Her eyes landed on a smiling, life-sized, inflatable dolphin floating a few feet from the pool's edge. Bingo.

She dropped her pool bag, walked to the edge,

and leaned forward, straining to grab the dolphin that seemed to be laughing at her as it managed to stay about six inches out of reach. "Gotta say, I'm a little surprised a bachelor has a pool full of inflatable zoo animals."

"Party supplies. I knew the kids would love them," Ethan said from behind her. "Not sure what I'm going to do with them now though. Maybe I'll put them in one of the guest rooms."

"I guess that's better than an inflatable doll," Claire responded, eyeing the dolphin. She could probably reach the darn thing if she got on her hands and knees. But taking the classic doggy-style position on the pool deck with Ethan somewhere behind her felt like a desperate cry for attention.

Instead, she dangled her toes an inch over the edge of the pool and stretched a tiny bit farther. A heart-stopping instant later, she felt her equilibrium shift forward—sending her face-first toward the deep end of the pool.

Letting out a strangled yelp, Claire flared her arms in an attempt to regain balance before she splashed into the water. Her white dress was about to provide an unplanned peep show. Crap. Doggy style would have been less provocative.

A moment later, a strong arm wrapped around her waist and hauled her back, bumping her to a stop against a warm, naked male chest. She gripped Ethan's forearm, tipped her head back to rest on his shoulder, and laughed with relief. "I owe you one, Lucky. This dress was a second away from transparency."

"Damn." He chuckled, his voice low and sexy against her temple. "I didn't think that one through."

Keeping her locked against his chest, he took a few steps back and to the right, guiding her into the darkness created by the shadow of the waterfall. He brushed her hair from the side of her face and slowly slid it over her left shoulder. "I've wanted to do this all night."

He dipped his head to her exposed neck and ran his tongue from her collarbone to the exquisitely sensitive spot behind her ear. Moaning deep in her throat, Claire tipped her head to the left and arched her back, pushing her breasts against the restraining fabric of her dress. Heat and need spiraled through her. In an embarrassingly short amount of time, his skilled mouth's attention had her squirming in his arms.

"Have to stop," she panted. "Mom … kids … inside."

"Haven't forgotten," he grunted, trailing his mouth down her neck. "I'd be doing a hell of a lot more than kissing your neck if we were alone." He slipped a hand up to cup the underside of one breast, skimmed a thumb over her nipple, and whispered what he wanted to be doing to her right now.

Claire felt her eyes go glassy and her bones melt away. Thankfully, Ethan still had her manacled against him since his sexy promises of pleasure left her too weak to stand on her own. She'd never been into dirty talk, but Ethan's vivid description of what they could do together didn't sound dirty—it just sounded like a really, really good idea.

When she felt him take a shaky breath and step away, she let out a needy little whimper in disappointment, missing the feel of him pressed along her back.

"Time to cool off," Ethan said wryly, stepping past her to dive into the pool's depths.

"Holy smokes," she muttered, touching a trembling hand to where Ethan had kissed her neck. As the thick sexual haze clouding Claire's mind began to clear, she was both grateful and a little surprised that Ethan had been the one mature and responsible enough to stop making out before they got busted.

For the next few minutes, he tossed all remaining toys out of the pool and she stacked them in the semi-sheltered area alongside the waterfall. Claire didn't look at him, and neither of them spoke while they worked. The tranquil sound of chirping crickets and rolling waves filled the silence, giving them both a moment to "cool off" as Ethan had put it.

More importantly, Claire needed to remain cooled off for the foreseeable future. They'd just rounded second base while his mom and her kids were inside the house. Even though they'd been hidden in the dark shadows of the landscaping, it still rattled her how easily she could get carried away with him. What would they have done if they'd been alone?

The memory of Ethan's whispered words shot a jolt of excitement and longing through her that negated any cooling off she'd managed to achieve. *Sheesh*. She was really losing her grip, and as a single mom, tumbling over the edge wasn't an option.

Claire deposited a slowly deflating sea turtle on top of the pile of creatures and blew a few strands of hair from her face. Hands on her hips, she faced her tempting-as-sin faux beau. He braced his hands on the edge of the pool and boosted himself from the water. His muscles contracted at the effort, sending streams of moonlit water sluicing down the deep contours between each defined ab.

Eyes locked on the glorious sight, she mumbled a curse and swallowed hard. Not having sex might sound like a logical idea, but her willpower around Ethan tended to deflate faster than the sad, droopy sea turtle behind her. In all honesty, she'd likely jump him right now if they were alone.

When she finally tore her gaze from those abs— *oh God, those abs*—she found him studying her with a knowing smile. "You want me bad," he teased, a devilish gleam lighting his eyes.

She shook her head. "Not gonna happen." Sure, she said it more for her sake than his, but saying it out loud gave it more staying power, right?

His smile widened at the unintentional challenge.

Claire grunted. She really had to quit provoking his competitive nature. "I mean it, Lucky; this has got to remain a business deal. I appreciate your help, but I refuse to get swept away in some whirlwind romance that's going to leave me dizzy, flat on my ass, and full of regret when it's over."

"What do you have against romance?"

"How about the fact that it's predominately used by men as a way to get laid?"

He blinked in surprise, then lifted a stray towel from the back of the chair and slung it across his shoulders. Gripping each end of the towel with a strong hand, he eyed her with an assessing expression. "Okay," he eventually conceded with a small nod. "I promise not to use romantic gestures with you to get laid."

She opened her mouth to argue, then snapped it

shut when she realized she had nothing to argue about. He'd calmly listened to her concern and offered a course of action to lessen that concern. As long as he stuck to his word and she limited their alone time to a bare minimum, she just might be strong enough to keep her hands off him.

Meanwhile, this promised to be the longest, most sexually frustrating pretend relationship of her flipping life.

TEN

"THE owner's box?" Claire asked, bringing their group of four to a sudden stop outside the door to the luxury suite. "I assumed you'd have access to good tickets. I didn't realize we'd be rubbing elbows with the top brass."

Ethan noted the inquisitive tilt to Claire's head. She didn't look upset, concerned, or even excited to find out they'd be watching the game with the team's owner, simply curious. He'd planned to sit in standard seats, then Harrison Dasher had intervened.

"When Dasher heard I'd be at the game with you guys, he asked us to join him."

"Who's Dasher?" Ty asked, looking at his mom.

"Mr. Dasher owns the team," Claire supplied, making eye contact with Ty and Grace. "He's being generous to offer us such wonderful seats. I think it's best if we thank him and Ethan for the experience. Don't you agree?"

While both kids nodded, Ty looked up at him like he'd saved the world from alien invasion while winning the World Cup. A slight twinge of guilt hit Ethan's gut.

He'd planned the day with optimal kid enjoyment in mind. They'd spent hours at the zoo on a private VIP tour with one of the zookeepers providing behind-the-scenes information and access. Grace had jumped and bounced and clapped and twirled and smiled the entire time. Ethan didn't know a ton about nine-year-old girls, but he guessed she'd crash in the backseat on the ride home.

After the zoo, they'd arrived at the stadium well before game time. Not that he needed to wait for the gates to open. He knew all the security staff by first name and had been welcomed in with warm smiles, handshakes, and pleas to return. Unfortunately, the team hadn't found a solid striker to replace him yet. Rather than looking to the future, most fans seemed convinced enticing him back to the team provided their best chance at winning.

He'd graciously reminded them of his retirement and led Claire, Ty, and Grace to the locker room. While the girls waited outside, he'd introduced Ty to the team and gotten each of the players to sign a jersey for him. He'd wanted Claire's kids to like him. Judging by the awe in Ty's expression, he'd shot right past "like" and had landed somewhere between "adore" and "idolize."

His guilt intensified. Had he crossed a line? Christ, he didn't know. He'd never dated a single mom before. Was winning her kids over a dirty trick or a decent thing to do?

"Thank you, Ethan. This has been the best day of my life!" Ty clutched the jersey to his chest. "And the game hasn't even started yet!"

"Yeah. Thanks, Ethan." Grace gave him an unexpected hug around his waist. "Helping feed the animals at the zoo was the coolest thing ever!"

Ethan's heart swelled. He literally felt his frigging

heart expand in his chest. Was that even physically possible? "You're welcome," he managed, forcing the words past the sudden lump of emotion in his throat. He patted Grace's little back and raised his gaze to Claire's.

"Thank you," she mouthed, a range of emotions playing across her features. While her smile looked genuine, her eyes held a trace of weary resignation that didn't sit well with him.

He held her gaze in question. Instead of telling him what was bothering her, Claire nodded toward the door to the suite. "We should go in before more fans swarm you with selfie and autograph requests."

When Grace dropped her arms from his waist, he swung the door open and motioned inside. "Lead the way, guys," he said to the kids. "We're a few minutes early, but there should be tons of food, drinks, and candy set up in there already. I'm sure Mr. Dasher won't mind if you help yourselves to some."

Ty sucked in an excited breath and headed through the door, Grace on his heels.

As Claire stepped forward to follow inside, Ethan held the door with one hand and touched his fingertips to her hip with the other to stop her briefly before going in. "What's wrong?" he asked quietly.

"Nothing." Her one-word response didn't sound bitter or ticked or disappointed. Instead, Claire sounded oddly distant even though she stood less than a foot away.

"I'm not buying it. There's a shadow in those beautiful blue-green eyes. You can either tell me what's wrong, or I can start making wild assumptions." He shrugged. "Probably a lot safer and healthier for both of us if you just tell me."

"Sorry." She licked her bottom lip and looked around to make sure no one was within earshot. "I keep forgetting how perceptive you are, and to be honest, I'm not used to talking about my feelings."

He cocked an eyebrow. In his experience, women loved to talk about their feelings. Something that had always worked in his favor in relationships since his mom had been adamant he would learn healthy communication skills. Which seemed really ironic considering they hardly spoke anymore.

"It's not that I can't talk about my feelings," she added. "It's more that Jack didn't want to hear about them, so I stopped sharing. And that sounded way more pathetic than I intended," she said with a self-conscious chuckle. "I'm having a great time today, Ethan. We all are." She gestured to the far wall where Ty and Grace were topping individual bowls of popcorn with candy. "I really appreciate the day you've planned for us and how great you've been with the kids."

"But … ?" Ethan prompted, seeing the apology in her eyes.

"But I'm worried if I'm not careful, they're going to get hurt in all this."

"We're."

Claire scrunched up her cute little nose in confusion. "Huh?"

"You said 'if I'm not careful' but it's not all on your shoulders. We're both responsible for making sure they don't get hurt."

Her eyes softened. "Thank you," she whispered, resting her palm on his chest for a beat. "The more I know you, the more I'm sure that I'm the lucky one." She kissed his cheek and stepped into the room.

Ethan stood in the doorway, his skin tingling where Claire's hand and lips had been. He watched her gracefully make her way across the otherwise empty room to check on Ty and Grace. She smiled in playful delight as she listened to the culinary combinations they'd created with popcorn and candy toppers. She kissed first Ty and then Grace on top of the head. Upon their animated encouragement, she picked up a plate to make her own creation.

Ethan's heart thudded a little oddly in his chest. He wasn't used to the crazy range of emotions she provoked in him. He could easily understand the times his blood burned with the need to drive her wild with the same desire and need she ignited in him. Right now, though, his chest expanded with other desires. He wanted to make her laugh when she was stressed, or see her face light up when she looked him, or feel her sigh against him when he wrapped his arms around her. He wanted more than sex. He wanted to be close to her—to be special to her.

"Christ, DuBois, my assistant said you were bringing a woman and two kids to the match. I assumed you were trying to get laid by scoring major points with some single mom, but you're looking at her like a goddamn puppy without a home."

Ethan drew in a slow, fortifying breath and turned to face the team's dynamic and often outspoken owner, Harrison Dasher. "It's good to see you, Dasher." Ethan extended his hand to the dark-haired, hard-faced man.

Dasher took his hand in a firm grip. "You could

see me a hell of a lot more often if you stopped playing hard to get. The team needs you, DuBois."

"I'm the past. The team needs to look to the future. You have two under-twenties with massive potential if the coach would give them the playtime they deserve. Now, come on." Ethan stepped into the room and nodded toward Claire and the kids. "I'll introduce you."

He heard Dasher heave out a sigh behind him. At barely forty years old, Dasher held multiple degrees from some of the world's best universities, ran a massively successful investment corporation, and sat on the board of multiple charitable foundations. Dasher was rich, powerful, and as used to getting his way as normal people were used to getting lunch.

Ethan had weighed the pros and cons of coming to the game today. Though he'd wanted to impress Claire and the kids with his connections and the star power he still wielded in the soccer world, he'd known Dasher's pressure to return to the team would be a major pain in the ass. Right or wrong, his desire to give Claire, Ty, and Grace an experience no one else could, had tipped the scales.

"Dasher," he said, reaching Claire's side, "this is Claire Bennett and her kids, Ty and Grace."

Ethan watched as both kids did a great job shaking hands and politely thanking Dasher for the tickets. The hard-ass looked impressed by their manners which made Ethan smile with pride. His smile changed to a scowl when Dasher lingered over his handshake with Claire, masculine appreciation flashing across his face.

"The match just started. You guys can watch

from the seats if you want," Ethan said to the kids. He wrapped an arm around Claire's waist and pointed to the box seats on the opposite side of a large sliding glass door.

Ty slid the door open, letting in the familiar stadium sounds of the crowd chanting and clapping to the beat of a pounding drum. Nostalgia tugged at him. No other sport sounded quite like the Beautiful Game.

Once both kids were seated on the opposite side of the glass, Ethan turned to Dasher. "I'm surprised none of your other guests have arrived yet. Whenever I looked up at this box from the field, it was spilling over with people."

"I uninvited them when I heard you were coming. We need to talk, and you're not returning my phone calls."

Ethan ground his jaw and sucked in a deep breath before answering. "I've told you. I'm retired. There's nothing more we need to talk about."

"Goddammit, DuBois, you've got me by the balls. We can't win the championship without a world-class striker. What the hell do you want? More money? A new coaching staff? A piece of my soul?"

"I'd like you to look up the word 'retired' because you sure as hell don't understand what it means."

"You're twenty-nine, and you play like you're five years younger. No way in hell you're actually retired. I heard you were spotted on a flight to London a couple of months back. You better not be going to some damn European club." He glared at Ethan.

"Retired," Ethan repeated.

Dasher snorted, then turned a charming smile on Claire. "Can I get you a drink? I suggest something strong if you have to deal with this frustrating bastard."

A sexy, low laugh rumbled from Claire's throat. "A glass of white would be nice while I enjoy the show."

Dasher glanced toward the field. "Yeah. Should be a good matchup. Kansas City always plays to win." He poured a glass of wine and extended it not quite far enough for Claire to reach it.

"I was talking about the show in here," she said, stepping away from Ethan to take the wine from Dasher. "You two sound like an old bickering couple. Not that I mind. In fact, you make my conversations at work seem healthy in comparison."

Dasher chuckled. "That's not fair. I bet you don't have to deal with professional athletes. A bunch of divas, all of them." He took a step closer and eyed Claire with an intensity that made Ethan's fists clench. The asshole had frigging maneuvered it so Claire was now standing next to him instead of Ethan.

"What you'd say your last name was, beautiful?"

"Bennett." She sipped her wine.

"As in Bennett Industries?" He cocked an eyebrow in recognition.

"Claire runs the place," Ethan offered with pride.

"I'm impressed."

"Don't be." She shrugged. "None of my siblings wanted the job."

"She's being modest." Ethan stepped closer and took her free hand in his. Holding her gaze, he raised their joined hands and brushed a kiss to the back of her hand. "Claire's a natural leader."

"Beautiful, smart, and rich," Dasher mused. "I'm starting to understand why you're refusing to return. But you still have a few great years left in you, DuBois. I hope you don't regret sitting on the sidelines when you could've been centerfield, leading your teammates to a championship."

Ethan felt Claire tense beside him. He gave her hand a reassuring squeeze, knowing it was time to end this argument before Dasher planted any more doubt in her mind. "I gave you a lot of great years," he said, finality in his tone. "Hell, I may have given you my best years. It's time we both move on."

"Shit," Dasher groaned. "Now you really do sound like my ex-wife." He walked to the bar and grabbed a beer from the ice bucket. "Bunch of divas," he mumbled, taking a swig.

Chuckling, Ethan walked with Claire to the glass door dividing the suite from the box seats. He slid the door open, slung an arm across her shoulders, and pulled her to his side as they stood watching the game below. God, she felt great settled against him—warm and soft and so damn feminine it made his gut ache.

"You're on TV!" Grace screamed in excitement, pointing to the giant jumbotron at the end of the field.

Ethan flashed a smile and waved at the camera pointed at them. The crowd cheered in response and began chanting his last name, a tradition that had started his first game at the stadium and been repeated after every goal he ever scored there.

He felt Claire laughing beside him. "What did I get myself into with you, DuBois?"

He grinned down at her. "Getting us on the jumbotron deserves a bonus, don't you think?"

Claire licked her lower lip and visibly swallowed. "Sounds fair. Did you have anything in mind?" she asked in a throaty whisper.

"A few things, actually," he murmured, leaning forward and brushing his lips across hers in a soft, playful kiss. When the crowd roared in approval, Claire giggled against his lips.

"Sorry," she said, fighting back laughter and dropping her head to his shoulder. "Kissing on the jumbotron is a new experience for me."

"How was it?"

"Unexpected. And honestly?" She tipped her head back to grin at him. "A little exhilarating."

"Kinda like me," he teased.

"Don't sell yourself short, Lucky," she sighed. "You're a whole lot of exhilarating."

Ethan dropped a kiss on top of her head, his blood humming with pleasure. Aside from Dasher's bellyaching, today couldn't have gone any better. He'd had a great time reaching his goal of maximum enjoyment for the kids.

It surprised him to realize how much he enjoyed being a part of the team Claire had built with her kids. And the more time he spent with the three of them, the more he realized he didn't want to be cut from their team anytime soon. Problem was, Claire had been right when they talked in her office. Never being one for sitting around, he'd started planning for the next stage of his life the moment he'd retired at the end of last season. And his plans involved staying in Silver Bay only long enough to make amends with his mom.

The time he spent with Claire and her kids made him question those plans. It sounded too damn cheesy to admit out loud, but it felt like being with them filled something inside him that he'd never realized was empty. Besides, did he really want to walk away from the rare woman who didn't see his fame and fortune as his most appealing quality?

The more he learned about her, the more he understood what a great fit they were. He'd always been a classic striker, on and off the field—charging, attacking, always moving forward and thinking about the future. Claire was a natural defender—containing risks, fixing problems, and remembering past mistakes to avoid making them again.

If he wanted a real chance with her, he needed to convince Claire they were right for each other. The way he figured it, he had from now until the bachelorette auction to get the job done. And while he wouldn't use romance to get laid, he had no problem using it to show Claire he could make her as happy as she made him.

So what if he'd never had to romance a woman before solely to convince her to go out with him on a non-pretend basis? He didn't mind hard work. Soccer had taught him a long time ago that the toughest goals to make were always the most rewarding.

ELEVEN

"NO flips!" Claire yelled to her kiddos as she sat with Hannah in her sunroom, watching Ty and Grace playing on the backyard trampoline.

It was Saturday afternoon, two weeks since their trip to Chicago, and Ethan was due to pick her up for their official weekend date in an hour. Not that they only saw each other on official dates.

The Monday after their trip to Chicago, Ethan had stopped by her office with flowers and a caffè mocha, her favorite drink from Hannah's coffee shop. The sweet gesture prompted her to invite him to dinner at her house that night. On Tuesday morning, he'd surprised her with chocolates and another caffè mocha and had invited her and the kids to dinner at his house as a thank you for Monday night's dinner.

The pattern had continued since then. He'd drop by her office with a treat or to go to lunch with her during the day, and they'd hang out with the kids in the evenings and over the weekend. They ate dinners together, watched movies, hiked, talked, laughed, boated, and played hours of card games, board games and Xbox. Over the past two weeks, her family of three had slipped so easily into being a family of four that Claire couldn't quite remember how they spent their time before Ethan was around.

But tonight was different. Tonight they'd be going out alone. Hannah, her babysitter for the evening, had arrived early for some sister-chat time before Claire headed out. They'd just finished talking about their brother Pax's upcoming wedding in Costa Rica when Claire's phone pinged with an incoming text.

"Say what now?" she mumbled, looking at her phone.

"What's up?" Hannah asked. "Last time I saw you look that surprised Kat had just labeled your new heels *F*-me shoes."

"I don't believe it." Claire gawked at her sister. "Ethan texted that he wants to take me for a ride along the beach tonight and that I should wear a tight outfit." She shook her head. "I must have misunderstood. He's a guy, but he's not a jerk. And they weren't *F*-me shoes," she snapped, yanking her phone closer to re-read his text.

"Yep. Clear as day. Skin-tight outfit was the main point of his text." She rubbed at the tension building in her temples with her fingertips. "Not sure how to respond to that."

"Kat would give him the middle-finger emoji," Hannah supplied in a helpful tone.

"And that would work for her. But I'm a little more ... " Claire watched Ty step to the side on the trampoline to clear space for Grace who had a very determined expression on her cute little face. Oh no. Claire knew that look. She stepped forward and raised her voice. "No flips," she reminded both kids through the open window in her authoritative, don't-even-try-to-argue-with-me mom voice. She turned back to Hannah. "I'm a little more, you know, mother-y," she finished. "The middle-finger emoji doesn't really suit me."

"Hmmm. How about the thinky-face one?" Hannah suggested.

"That would mean I'm considering it."

"Maybe you should."

Claire narrowed her eyes in a scowl. She liked Ethan. She really did. Didn't mean she planned to become his dress-up doll.

"Fine." Hannah raised her hands in surrender. "What are you going to do?"

She thought it over for a beat. "I'm going to send a mature, eloquent response expressing my decision to decline his suggestion."

"Thumbs-down emoji?" Hannah asked.

"Yep," Claire said, shooting off the text.

"Maybe you should at least put on something less"—Hannah waved her hand in an encompassing circle at Claire's sky-blue shift dress—"Sunday brunch-ish."

"Nope. Jack always tried to tell me what to wear. I didn't let him do it, and I'm not letting my pretend—" Claire bit her lips closed a second before she let her little secret slip. She cleared her throat. "My *pretentious* new boyfriend do it either."

Hannah made a face. "Ethan's not pretentious. From what I can tell, he's really sweet and isn't one of those guys who takes himself too seriously. You know," she said, dropping her voice, "like Jack."

True. Her ex epitomized pretension, while Ethan, a world-class athlete, never bragged or flaunted or even seemed to notice his utter awesomeness. *Ugh*. Now she felt crappy having called him pretentious, but it'd been the first word she could think of that started with "pretend."

"You're right," she conceded. "He's great. But I'm still not playing 'slutty makeover party' for him."

When the doorbell rang an hour later, Claire sauntered to her front door wearing her dress, strappy sandals, and a no-way-am-I-changing-for-you expression. She swung the door open and went hands-on-hips, bracing herself for a fight.

Wearing trim-cut cargo shorts and a navy-blue T-shirt made of slightly stretchy-looking athletic material, Ethan grinned at her. "Evening," he said as a way of greeting. He scanned his gaze down and then up her body—stopping briefly at the bare expanse of thigh below her dress and above her knees. His appraisal widened into a full-blown smile, kicking his dimples into action. "Are you sure you want to wear that dress? Don't get me wrong, it's a showstopper, but you might be more comfortable in something a little more ... Well, it could be difficult to ... you know ..." He trailed off, making a vague motion toward her lower body with his hand.

"I'm good," she repeated more firmly.

"Works for me." Sounding way more pleased than she expected, Ethan shrugged a shoulder and looked around her. "Hey, Hannah. You the sitter?"

"Yep."

"Great." He beamed at her. "I picked up a movie on the way over for you guys. No worries if you don't get around to watching it tonight. I'd told the kids about it at dinner a few nights ago, and they both said they'd like to see it, so I grabbed a copy in case you were looking for something to watch."

"That's so thoughtful," Hannah said, looking at Claire with an I-told-you-he-wasn't-pretentious head tilt. "What is it?"

"*The Princess Bride.*"

"Seriously?" Hannah went brows up. "I'm shocked you like that movie."

"What can I say?" He winked. "I'm a sucker for a happy ending."

Hannah took the movie from him. "Thanks. I haven't seen this in years. It'll be fun to watch with Ty and Grace." She tapped it absentmindedly against her palm. "So, what's on the docket for tonight's date?"

"Didn't Claire tell you?" He sounded surprised. "We're going for a bike ride along the shore. I know she loves to cycle."

Hannah shot her an amused, questioning look. "I guess she forgot to mention it."

Claire's mind raced through their previous conversations. He'd never said anything about a bike ride.

"I texted earlier and suggested she dress for a ride along the beach."

Oh. Holy. Smokes. He'd meant a bike ride? Claire opened her mouth to confess her misunderstanding. She needed to change.

"Silly me," Hannah interrupted, feigning forgetfulness. "Claire *did* tell me you guys were going for a ride. I suggested she put on something more appropriate"—as if sharing a secret, she shielded one side of her mouth and turned toward Ethan—"and a little less revealing. But she insisted on that dress."

Scanning her bare legs again, Ethan threw up his hands in a playful show of surrender. "Who am I to argue?" He shrugged and looked toward the backyard. "Before we leave, I'm going to say hi to Ty and Grace. Back in a minute."

Forcing a slightly manic smile past gritted teeth, Claire nodded her head up and down until Ethan cleared the room. "What the hell?" she turned to her nefarious sister.

"Couldn't help it," Hannah said, wiping away tears of silent, chest-shaking laughter. "The image of you trying to keep that dress down while you're riding all over town was too funny to resist."

Claire narrowed her eyes and pointed at Hannah. "Do you have any idea how hard it is going to be to ride a bike in this dress without flashing Ethan and everyone else in Silver Bay?"

"Yeah," Hannah said on another bubble of laughter. "But you kinda deserved it. Ethan planned a romantic date for you and simply suggested you wear something that wouldn't get caught in the bike's chain, and you thought the worst of him."

Claire crossed her arms. Though admittedly concerned about the feasibility of maneuvering her bike in the dress and maintaining a PG rating, she couldn't deny jumping to conclusions about Ethan's text. Guess she still had a few issues to work through from her past. "Fine," she said on a heavy sigh. "I deserved it."

"Don't look so glum. If anyone can look refined and graceful biking in a short dress, it's you, big sis."

Claire snorted. "Refined and graceful is shooting a little high. If I don't get arrested for indecent exposure, I'll consider tonight a success."

•••

Peddling along the flat bike path that hugged Lake Michigan's shoreline, Claire tugged at her dress. They'd been riding for twenty minutes as the September sun sank low on the horizon and a slight breeze blew in from the lake. So far she'd managed to keep from flashing Ethan or anyone else enjoying the path. Fingers crossed her luck would hold.

She glanced over her shoulder and noted the growing distance between her bike and his. Sure, she biked multiple times a week and could maintain a good pace even while fighting her dress from turning into a sail, but she shouldn't be pulling away from him this easily.

Why the heck did he keep slipping farther and farther behind?

"You doing okay back there?" Claire tossed the words over her shoulder.

"Yeah," he grunted in a strained voice.

She slowed down until he reached her side. "Do you need to take a break? You look really sweaty." Claire coasted beside him.

"Not much farther," he panted. "Just need to make it around the bend."

Five minutes later, Ethan pulled his bike to the side of the path, grabbed his water, and chugged half the bottle. Claire parked her bike next to his, smoothed out her dress, and studied him with growing confusion. He'd retired from professional soccer less than a year ago, and his lean, chiseled body looked strong, healthy, and capable of performing at maximum levels of exertion. So how come he was acting like he'd just finished a marathon rather than a casual bike ride?

She watched as he paced in circles, huffing and puffing, trying to get his heart rate under control. Something wasn't adding up. She dropped her gaze to his bike. "Where'd you get your ride?"

"It's an old one from high school."

"Let me take a look." She tucked her flyaway dress tight around her thighs and crouched next to the tired-looking bike to search for anything that seemed off. When she reached the back wheel, she realized that something wasn't off—it was on. "Your break is stuck."

Ethan crouched down, only inches from her side. She could feel the heat rising from his body and smell the scent of male skin slick with sweat. She imagined he'd smell the same after a vigorous love-making session ... or two.

She cleared her throat. "Looks like you've been riding with your back break engaged."

"Yeah, the son of a bitch locked up a few miles back."

"Huh?" Her thoughts were still more on beds than bikes. God, even his sweat smelled good. Key body parts tightened. She forced herself to focus. "Why didn't you stop?"

Ethan turned to look at her. "If I stopped every time I hit a little resistance in life, I wouldn't get anywhere." He rose to his feet and offered her his hand and a devilish grin. "Come on. I have a surprise for you."

Claire made a face and studied him for a heavy beat before taking his hand. "I hate surprises," she admitted as he helped her to her feet.

"I bet you'll like my surprises," he teased, slinging an arm over her shoulder and leading her onto the beach.

"You mean like the time I found out you weren't Deb's cousin, or when I discovered you're a famous soccer player instead of a slacker, or when I realized you're younger than me and my son's coach, or—"

"Those were misunderstandings. Surprises are much better," he said, directing her down the beach toward a rocky outcrop near the water's edge about fifty yards away.

She made a noncommittal sound in the back of her throat. They'd have to agree to disagree on that one.

Ethan chuckled, pulled her tighter to him, and dropped a kiss on top of her head. It felt good to be wrapped under his arm, enveloped by his heat and strength. She felt both sexy and safe—a nice combination as it turned out.

Claire drew in a deep breath of brisk autumn air. "Fall is my favorite time of year," she said, hoping some small talk about the season would distract her from the feel of him pressed to her side.

"Mine too."

"Really?" She smiled, pleased. "What do you like best? The color of the leaves? The chill in the air? The smell of fires burning and pumpkin bars baking?"

He gave her a sheepish look. "It's the best time of year to play soccer. Winter is snowy, spring is wet, and summer is hot. Of course, I had to practice hours a day in all types of weather. But it's always better to play in good conditions."

She wrinkled her nose. "Choosing a favorite season shouldn't be so pragmatic."

"Reality taught me to be practical, even as a kid."

"You worked hard?"

"I didn't have the natural ability other teammates were born with. I had to work hard to keep up." His matter-of-fact tone held no emotion, suggesting neither bitterness nor pride over the statement.

Claire executed a dramatic eye roll. At over six feet of sculpted muscle, he looked like a modern-day Adonis. Who was he trying to kid? If he were any more naturally gifted, he'd be lethal. "Yeah. You're really pathetic," she deadpanned.

"That hurts," he said, sounding way too happy to mean it.

She bumped her shoulder against his arm. "You know I'm kidding."

"Are you sure? I can think of a few fun ways to convince you of my manliness."

A strangled laugh of nervous energy slipped from her lips. Okay, she sounded a tad hysterical. At least she was controlling herself better than Sherlock, her neighbor's overly friendly labradoodle, who had a latching-on-to-legs problem.

When they reached the outcrop, Ethan jumped onto a knee-high rock and turned back to hold out his hand.

She eyed his hand then her dress, and blew out a sigh. "Next time you make a clothing suggestion, I'm so going to listen," she mumbled, giving him her hand.

"It's good to know you're starting to trust me." He boosted her onto the rock.

Still holding her hand, he led her up and around a few more boulders, pointing out where she should step in a few tricky areas. After a few minutes of navigating the rocks, he dropped into a sandy alcove about the size of a small bedroom. The niche—surrounded by rock walls on three sides and Lake Michigan on the other—contained a large blue-checked blanket, picnic basket, multiple candles, and a bottle of her favorite wine artfully arranged in its center.

"Did I surprise you?" he asked, turning to look at her.

Claire froze, eyeing the most romantic setting she'd ever seen in her life. He'd done this for her. He'd cared enough about her to—

Stop! she yelled silently at her stupid, romantic heart. Her resistance had simply sparked his competitive nature, driving him to fight for what she said he couldn't have. This elaborately constructed date was about winning. That was all. It didn't make him a bad guy; it just made him … a guy.

Claire bit down hard on the inside of her lip and managed to resist a full body sigh.

Where were they? And she didn't mean their secluded alcove in the sand. Her relationship with Ethan confused her more than a fifty-page document from legal. She honestly didn't know where they stood anymore.

Were they pretend dating or actually going out? Was he only in this for the thrill of the hunt, likely to move on once she slept with him? Or did he want something more from her? If so, what? And even if he did want something more, did she have anything more to give him?

She'd not been able to make a relationship work with the father of her children. What made her think she could make one work with a hot, young soccer star, or any man for that matter? Jack might be right.

Maybe she was too controlling and independent to share her life with a partner.

And maybe she should have swallowed her pride and let Kat auction her off on a pity date. At least then she would know exactly where she stood with the guy.

Who would have thought hiring a pretend boyfriend would cause so much real confusion in her life? Technically, she might not be paying Ethan, but he knew that was the idea. And *she* knew business and pleasure mixed as well as oil and water. So why had she thrown the two together in a small town like Silver Bay and shook the heck out of them anyway?

They were never going to blend. Now she'd have to wait for things to settle down before she could clear out all the little chunks of business floating around in her personal life.

Rubbing the heart-shaped pendant hanging around her neck, she drew in a breath and looked down at Ethan to find him waiting for her response. "Yeah, Ethan, you surprised me. And not just tonight," she admitted and gave a long exhale.

He grabbed her hips and lowered her to stand beside him in the sand, his hands warm where they lingered.

"And that's bad because … ?" He studied her with a serious expression.

"If I'm surprised, it usually means I don't understand what's going on. That doesn't sit well with me." She looked down at the blanket, candles, picnic basket, and bottle of wine. "And I really don't understand what's going on. No one can see us tucked away down here, so this can't be for show."

"You still think I'm using romance to get laid?"

"No." Claire shook her head. "You promised me you wouldn't, and I trust you. But I can't help feeling"—she cringed in apology—"suspicious. Like you have an ulterior motive."

"I'd say it's more a product of changing goals." He shrugged.

"I don't follow what you mean."

"Since I'm a guy, I'll use a sports analogy to explain. When I first found out LA was considering me, all I wanted to do was make the team. So I fought hard to prove that I deserved a chance. Once I was on the team, my goal shifted from getting a spot on the roster to securing a starting position. Once I did that, I worked at upping my goals scored as well as becoming a leader on the field to make myself as indispensable as possible."

"And how does that apply to this?" She gestured to the romantic little alcove.

"When I first met you, pretending to be your boyfriend sounded like an entertaining diversion so I agreed to help out. After I got to know you, my goal changed. This"—he copied her sweeping gesture of the sandy nook—"is me showing you that I'm not pretending anymore." He tilted his head, considering. "Not sure I ever really was."

She sucked in a breath as panic sliced through her. "But this was supposed to be a business deal." The words tumbled out before she could conceal the hysteria edging her voice.

The corner of his lips tilted up in a knowing smile. "For me, this was never about business." He trailed his thumb down her jawline. "You're special to me, Claire." He skimmed his fingertips down her arm and took her hand in his. "I planned tonight to show you that."

"I'm sorry." Her stomach twisted in a giant knot of guilt. "When I propositioned you in that bar, I never meant for any of this to happen."

"Are you sorry it did?"

She shook her head and blew out a sigh. "No. Which makes me feel even guiltier. I like being with you. A lot. But I know whatever is going on between us is temporary. I don't want anyone to end up hurt when it's over."

"Like when your marriage ended?"

"No." Claire gave a humorless chuckle and drew back in surprise. "Even though everyone assumes the divorce devastated me, it didn't."

Ethan tugged her hand to lead her to the blanket. "We've danced around the subject for weeks. Now seems like a good time to tell me about your marriage over a glass of wine." He sat down on the blue-checked blanket and started opening the bottle of red next to him.

Still standing, Claire chewed her lip and watched him efficiently remove the cork and fill two wine glasses set on top of the closed picnic basket. With a persuasive smile, he lifted one glass toward her and patted the spot next to him.

"Fine," she said on an exhale and carefully maneuvered into a sitting position with her legs bent and tucked beside her in the short dress. "What do you want to know?"

"Anything you're willing to tell me."

Staring at the calm water, she sipped the wine he handed her and thought for a moment before answering. "I met Jack at one of my mom's charity functions when I was home for the summer before my last year of college. He was eight years older than me, suave, and sophisticated. I'd only dated college guys before him. In comparison, his serious manner seemed so mature." She gave a humorless chuckle. "I didn't realize how restricting it would feel once the romance wore off." She drew in a breath and shook her head. "Anyway, we dated through the summer and then long-distance during my senior year. He proposed the day I graduated, and we were married by fall. Ty came along just under a year later and Grace thirteen months after Ty. We were married for seven years when Jack filed for divorce. That was almost four years ago now, but it seems like another lifetime."

"Why'd you get divorced?"

"To correct the mistake we made by getting married in the first place." She swirled the glass of wine in her hand and stared at the spinning scarlet liquid.

"What made it a mistake?" Ethan asked gently.

"A lot of things. Me being so young, our age gap, our short engagement, his personality, my personality. Looking back, I can see a ton of signs that our marriage wouldn't work. But the allure of romance blinded me to them." She drained her glass of wine.

"Claire ... " Ethan waited until she turned to meet his gaze. "Did the bastard cheat on you?"

"No." She set her glass back on top of the picnic basket. "Gemma works as a receptionist in one of the doctor's offices Jack calls on. He met her after our divorce and fell instantly, magically in love." Somehow she managed not to roll her eyes. "Apparently, Gemma refused to date him at first.

She thought he should focus on his kids after the divorce." Claire smiled at the memory. "At the time, I didn't think much about her refusal to jump into a relationship with Jack. Looking back, I have to give her credit. She made him take it slow until she was sure it was okay with Ty and Grace."

"And what about you? Was it okay with you?"

"At first, I admit my pride was stung. He dumped me and replaced me within a year."

"And you haven't dated since the divorce."

"Some." She shrugged. "Nothing serious. Work and the kids keep me busy."

"Once bitten, twice shy?"

She took a deep breath, choosing her next words carefully. "Dating often leads to marriage. I'm not sure that's the right path for me to go down again." Claire dropped eye contact, slipping off her sandals, and scooting to the edge of the blanket to dig her toes in the sand. "Some people are better on their own."

"I disagree," Ethan said. "Every victory is sweeter and every loss is easier when you're part of a team. It's true in sports and in life."

"Marriage isn't a game." She turned to meet his eyes again.

"No, but it involves teamwork and trust. When I was playing, there were games where I couldn't connect with the goal to save my life. On those days, I had to trust my teammates to carry me on their backs. And I let them because I knew I'd do the same for them the next day, or next week, or next month. That kind of support comes from being on a team."

"Maybe you're the one who should get married,

Lucky." Claire summoned a teasing smile, hoping his nickname would lighten the mood. "Or maybe you could join a rec soccer team at the community center. Or a book club. Or a knitting group. Or—"she tilted her head in question—"you could return to your old club and adoring fans for a bucketload of money."

She picked up her empty glass and extended it toward him. "Why don't you give me a refill, and we can make a pros and cons list for each option?"

Ethan sighed and filled her glass. "Why doesn't anyone believe I'm actually retired?"

Claire took a sip of wine and stared at the waves lapping onto the shore in front of them. Soothed by both the lulling sound of the water and the slow slide of the red wine into her system, she considered his question. "Because most people can only dream about being a professional athlete, and they can't imagine walking away from that dream if they had the choice to stay," she mused, keeping her words quiet and contemplative rather than combative.

"Maybe I have a new dream, a new goal." Intensity edged his voice, making him sound unusually serious, solemn even.

Legs stretched out in front of him, he reclined back on the blanket and propped himself upright on his elbows. He stared back at her with those penetrating blue eyes that seemed to see all the way to her soul.

"Care to share what that new goal is?" She sounded breathless, which didn't surprise her. Ethan had always been able to take her breath away, even on that first night in the bar.

The corners of his lips curled slightly upward,

and his eyes lit with an emotion she couldn't read. "Not yet." He held her gaze as one, two, three languid waves rolled to shore. "But soon."

Holy smokes. Her heart raced. Even though the temperature had dropped with the setting sun, she felt flushed.

"Now, let's eat," he said, his voice regaining its normal carefree tone. "I need to load up on carbs before attempting to ride back on the bike from hell. Or"—he looked at her with boyish earnestness— "do you think your bike's handlebars could hold you? I could give you a ride."

"Nope." She shook her head, slow and emphatic. "Not going to happen. If I rode into Silver Bay on *those* handlebars in *this* dress, I'd be the talk of the town before we even reached my street."

Ethan's face brightened with a megawatt, dimple-activating smile. "Not a problem. I'll ride on the handlebars, and you can pedal."

Claire snorted a laugh and rolled her eyes. "That would cause an even bigger scene. How about I disengage your locked brake so you can ride your own bike?"

Ethan blew out an exaggerated sigh and started digging food out of the picnic basket. "My idea would have been a lot more fun."

"You're an international soccer star. You're used to being the center of attention. I'm not." She unwrapped a bowl of chilled, fresh-cut fruit that he pulled from the basket. "I've watched your highlight reel. The crowd's reaction when you scored the game-winning goal in the first-round World Cup match a few years ago blew me away. Women were shrieking. Grown men were crying. Everyone seemed to be chanting your name and cheering like you'd just saved the planet from a zombie apocalypse."

"Yeah." Without pausing or even looking up from rummaging the picnic basket, Ethan chuckled. "That felt good."

"Good?" Her voice shot up an octave. "You gave the entire nation something to celebrate, to be proud of. That would feel pretty freaking amazing to me, and I'm rarely a fan of attention."

He stilled and looked up at her with a lopsided grin. "Okay. Yeah. It did feel pretty freaking amazing."

Toying with the heart-shaped pendant around her neck, she tilted her head in question. "Aren't you going to miss it?"

"Nah," Ethan said, pulling a decadent-looking chocolate torte from the picnic basket. "There are a lot of pretty freaking amazing experiences out there. Care to share one with me?" His voice was playfully seductive as he extended the torte toward her.

Claire eyed the dessert and licked her lips. "Absolutely," she breathed.

In a flash of movement, the torte went flying. A second later, Ethan snagged an arm around her waist and toppled her onto the blanket, beneath him.

"I meant the chocolate dessert, you big lug," she said, laughing and playfully squirming beneath the muscled weight of his body.

"Oh, my mistake." Only inches away, Ethan grinned down at her with a wicked, teasing look in his gorgeous blue eyes. "Should we eat, then?" He pushed upward, a few inches away from her chest, as one of his large thighs slipped between both of hers.

The delicious weight and pressure of his leg made Claire squirm for an entirely different reason now.

She let out a soft moan of pleasure and gripped his arms to hold him in place. "No. Stay. I like you there. Right there," she said, unable to resist arching against him. Holy smokes. Maybe she was as bad as her randy neighbor dog after all.

"I like—no, scratch that," he said in a rough voice. "I love being *right there* too." He dipped his head to claim her mouth in a teasing, coaxing kiss. "Actually," he murmured between kissing, licking, nibbling her mouth, jawline and neck, "it's killing me that I'm not even closer to you *right there*."

"Mmm," she moaned and tightened her grip on him. The thought of him being *right there* over and over and over again stole her ability to form coherent words.

"But a promise is a promise." He rolled off of her, landing on his back beside her with a muttered curse. "No romance to get laid."

"What? Oh. Yeah. Okay. Right," she panted next to him. "Smart decision. Very mature. Very responsible."

Ethan's chest rumbled with laughter. "Glad you think so. Right now, I'm not sure if I should be proud of myself or pissed off at my own idiocy for making that promise."

She clamped her mouth shut before she could blurt out the truth—that for once in her life she ached to toss mature and responsible into the lake. Every fiber of her wanted to make crazy, passionate love on that blue blanket in the sand until Ethan didn't have the strength to stand, let alone ride that bike of his back into town.

He pushed himself into a sitting position. "We should probably move this picnic closer to the bike path. A highly visible, well-lit spot … " He scanned down the length of her body and then back up, locking his overheated gaze with hers. "Before it's too late."

She wanted to push his shoulders backward to the ground, straddle him, and kiss him until the heat she saw in his eyes exploded into searing passion. The instinct to touch him threatened to overwhelm all rational thought.

Damn. She needed to get a grip. Forcing back the disorienting desire, Claire pushed her dress down from its hiked position around her waist, stood, and walked toward the lake. She needed space to regroup.

Twenty steps away, at the point where dry sand turned to wet, she closed her eyes and drew in deep gulps of lakeshore air. The lap of the placid waves mingled with the clatter of Ethan behind her, tossing everything back into the basket, rushing to get them out of there "before it's too late."

But Claire recognized the emotion expanding her chest and stealing her breath and knew her stupid heart was starting to blur the line between romance, sexual desire, and love again. She wrapped one arm around her waist and gripped the pendant around her neck in her other hand. With a grounding breath, she fought against romance's hypnotic, intoxicating pull. Knowing firsthand the price of getting swept off her feet, Claire hoped liked crazy it wasn't already too late for her.

TWELVE

FINISHING his last set of lat pulldowns, Ethan bit back a grin as Logan glowered through the plate glass window at the group of gawkers clustered on the sidewalk in front of the gym.

"Every damn day," Logan groused, the glower now directed at Ethan—the reason for all the commotion. "Soccer Boy, I told you to work out in the back of the gym. I'm serious, mate. Whenever you're in the front window, you turn this place into a spectacle rather than a respectable workout establishment."

"Sorry, *mate*. My favorite machines are up front. Besides, I've only been in town a couple of months. Everybody will settle down once they get used to seeing me around."

"Way I hear it, you're not going to be sticking around long enough for that to happen."

Ethan stood up from the machine and grabbed his water bottle. "I've heard that too." He took a swig of water.

"Also heard your old team isn't doing well without you. Sounds like they're willing to pay some serious money to get you back." Logan narrowed his eyes. "I'd hate to see anyone around here get hurt when you waltz back to your old life." He stepped closer, displaying his height advantage.

Unfazed by the big Australian's pissy attitude, Ethan flashed him a cocky smile and stripped his shirt off to use as a towel to wipe away sweat. Flashes exploded outside the window, and one woman actually squealed in excitement.

"Christ," Logan groaned and shook his head. "I don't need the bodies of a bunch of swooning women blocking my doorway." He yanked the blinds closed, barring both the gawkers and the sunlight from the gym. "If any of my clients complain about working out in the dark, I'll tell them who to thank."

"Make you a deal," Ethan said. "I'll keep to the back of the gym until the town gets used to seeing me around if you'll help me with Claire."

Logan stiffened. "Thought you were already dating her. What do you need my help for?"

"I've tried to win her over with one romantic gesture after another. I've taken her on a sunset bike ride to a candlelit picnic dinner on a blanket in the sand. I've hand-delivered truckloads of flowers and chocolates. I stop by her office most mornings with her favorite coffee from Fresh. I've had her and the kids over for dinners that I actually cooked myself. We even watched *Titanic* and *Dirty Dancing* together."

"Christ." Logan grimaced. "This entire conversation is giving me a cramp in my ass. What'd you do, search 'how to be romantic' on YouTube?"

"Nope," Ethan replied with a smug smile. "I used wikiHow."

"You doing all this to sleep with her?"

"Hell, no. I'm doing this to show Claire she should keep me around. She's smart, funny, nice to everyone—even her ex and his new wife—dedicated to her family, and fiercely independent. It's obvious she doesn't need a man to be happy. Which means I have to convince her that even if she doesn't need me in her life, she wants me there anyway."

"For how long?"

"Forever."

"You're shitting me?" Logan asked, jerking back in shock.

"I'm serious. I've never met anyone like her before. She's the one. I know it in my gut. Her and her kids—we make a great team."

Logan cocked an eyebrow. "How long have you known her?"

"Almost two months." Ethan shrugged. "I'm a decisive guy. Always have been. First time I stepped on the pitch, I knew I wanted to be a professional soccer player. Nothing could've stopped me. Not my mother, the harsh Wisconsin climate, or even my own lack of natural talent. I just knew it was right, and I was willing to do whatever I had to do to make it happen. Feels the same way with Claire."

Logan grunted and eyed Ethan with a skeptical expression. "Never met a guy so willing to talk about love." He shoved a hand through his hair and muttered something about the cramp in his ass getting worse.

Grinning, Ethan tossed the sweaty shirt into his gym bag and grabbed a clean one. "I love her, man." He pulled the shirt on over his head. "I'm not ashamed to admit it just because I haven't known her long. How long did it take you to fall for Kat? A month or two tops, I bet."

The scowl on Logan's face made it clear Ethan

had him on that one.

"Okay, Romeo," Logan said, blowing out a resigned breath. "If you're serious about making her happy, I'll help. What did you have in mind?"

"Excellent! I've got something big planned for next weekend. I'm going to need your help to pull it off. Or to be precise, I'm going to need your wife's help."

Logan chuckled. "You've got balls. I'll give you that." He slapped Ethan on the shoulder as he walked past him on the way to his office. "Word of warning. Kat's a tiger, and she'll do things her own way. You'll never be able to control her."

"I'm not trying to control anyone," Ethan said, raising his voice as Logan walked farther away.

"You sure of that?" Logan turned around to face him but kept walking backward toward his office. "You've told me all about what you want. Haven't heard you say what Claire wants. I reckon that means you either don't know or you don't care."

"I want to make her happy," Ethan snapped.

"What if getting rid of your ass makes Claire happy?" The big bastard shot Ethan an arrogant smile. "Would you really do anything for her even if it meant leaving her alone?"

A rare flash of anger burned through Ethan. "You don't know what the fuck you're talking about, *mate*."

Logan held up his hands in a don't-shoot gesture. "Not too long ago, I thought I knew what Kat wanted without bothering to ask her about it. Luckily, I came to my senses before I lost her for good." Logan smirked. "Can't help but wonder if you, Soccer Boy, are going to get so lucky."

•••

Pacing, Claire watched the street through the front window of her living room. The weeks she'd spent with Ethan since that first "soccer date" had flown by in a big, happy blur. It didn't seem possible that the bachelorette auction was only a week away. Once it was over, she had no clue where that would leave her and Ethan. You couldn't pretend date someone once the reason for the pretense was over, right?

Who was she kidding? She'd stopped pretending a long time ago, but that didn't mean they had any sort of a future together. She couldn't let her weakness for fairy-tale endings delude her into mistaking their romance for true love.

And, oh boy, had he romanced her. From flowers to candlelit dinners on the beach, Ethan kept one-upping himself. Not that she should have expected anything less. The night they'd met, Ethan had told her he only knew how to provide top-notch service—a statement he'd certainly proven true.

Tonight was their final date before their agreement ran out, and she had no idea what grand romantic gesture he had planned for her. Seriously. How do you top a candlelit sunset picnic on the beach? Even though it would be a challenge, Claire knew he'd find a way to exceed expectations—world-class competitors always did.

She wondered what Ethan would do if he realized her favorite times with him were the simple moments together doing stuff that felt real—that felt lasting. Would he change his tactics or would he press on with his all-things-romantic offensive drive?

Then again, real and lasting likely didn't interest him. If he planned to leave town once he worked things out with his mom, the short-term euphoria of romance might be all his schedule allowed. Which would make tonight their final date. Ever.

Pushing away the unsettling thought, Claire again wondered where they were going tonight. Ethan had refused to tell her what he'd planned. Too bad surprises didn't sit well with her. After a great deal of pestering on her part, he'd eventually fessed up to two details: they were going somewhere other than Silver Bay and she should wear a "nice dress."

After the bike-ride fiasco, she'd decided to follow his advice about her attire. Problem was, "nice dress" could be interpreted in a lot of different ways. Should she dress for a wedding? A country club? The theater? A fundraiser? A night of dancing? The ESPYS? She didn't know which stressed her out more—the idea of feeling overdressed or underdressed.

She'd literally tried on every single dress in her closet. She had a number of perfectly fine outfits to choose from. Her role at Bennett Industries often required she attend company award ceremonies, dinners, and charity functions. She also had a few special occasion dresses that would work for a semiformal or black-tie event, but they would look horribly out of place anywhere else.

She'd spent the entire day overthinking her options. Even at Ty's soccer match that afternoon, she'd spent more time talking to Deb about what dress she should wear than watching the game. Her straightforward friend had told her to stop being such a wuss and ask Ethan what the hell he meant by "nice." Unwilling to admit her ridiculous over-analysis of the situation to him, Claire had settled on a sleeveless black A-line with a matching black-and-white shrug. What it lacked in flare, it made up for in versatility. She tugged on the bottom corners of her shrug, wondering if she should leave it on or take it off.

Before she finished weighing the pros and cons of going sans shrug, a tingle of unease slipped down her spine and tightened the knot in her belly. She'd experienced similar feelings of foreboding in her past and knew better than to ignore them. Sure enough, when she glanced through the window again, a familiar black car was pulling to a stop in front of her house. *Oh crap.*

She hurried to her front door, knowing a show of strength to be her only hope. Straightening her shoulders, sensible shrug in place, she stepped onto her porch. The four doors of the car swung open, spilling a flurry of movement and excited chatter from the car. Like watching a tsunami approaching the shore, Claire braced herself and hoped for the best as the wave of feminine energy charged toward her.

Wearing stylish frayed jeans, a snug red tee, and an ornery grin, Kat led the pack with a garment bag draped over one arm. Directly behind her, dressed in vivid orange, tiny Mrs. Dobolek—the Bennett kids' childhood piano teacher—shuffled up the walk at an impressive speed. Looking more amused than enthusiastic, Hannah and Deb followed a few paces behind.

Claire might not be a professional athlete, but she'd always been a fan of sports and knew darn well that often the best defense was a good offense.

She summoned the no-nonsense tone she saved for stubborn employees or children or little sisters. "Kat, you're a mother now. You should be in a car with modern safety features, not joyriding around town in a beat-up old Buick."

"No worries. That new tank of an SUV Logan bought has a crap-load of airbags and every safety feature known to man." Kat waved off Claire's concern with a flick of her delicate wrist. "I rarely drive Bruno anymore. But I do take him out on special occasions. He has sentimental value." Kat looked fondly at her aging Buick. "He brought Logan and me together after all."

"I thought Mom finagled that?"

"It took a lot to bring us together. We were both very stubborn people."

"Were or are?" Claire asked dryly.

Kat grinned in response.

"Ladies." Claire forced a smile and looked at each woman in turn. "It's lovely of you to surprise me with a visit, but I was just about to step out. Would you be available to stop back tomorrow instead?"

"Oh, pumpkin. We heard about tonight's date with Mr. Sexy Soccer Man." Mrs. D shuffled closer and patted Claire's arm. "We're here to help, don't cha know." The older woman nodded her head with enough enthusiasm to actually jiggle her short, tight, heavily hair-sprayed gray curls.

Claire cringed. "I was afraid of that."

"We plan to save you from yourself." Kat eyed Claire up and down, shook her head in disgust, and stepped into the house. "Come on, ladies. We don't have much time."

Blowing out a sigh, Claire motioned the others inside. "Ethan will be here in less than an hour. I'm not sure what you're hoping to accomplish by then." She followed the group to her kitchen.

"We'll make this room the center of operations." Kat assumed command as if Claire hadn't said a damn word. "Mrs. D, you can sit at the kitchen table. You're in charge of keeping an eye on the time. Make sure to let us know when it's ten minutes to go-time. Can you handle that?"

"You betcha."

Kat turned to Hannah. "Sis, you can set up a makeup station there." She pointed to the kitchen island's far barstool and then focused on Deb. "You're in charge of finding the black *F*-me heels she's probably shoved into the back corner of her closet."

"What do they look like?" Deb asked.

"You'll know 'em when you see 'em."

"Got it." Deb practically saluted Kat before she charged from the room.

Traitor. Claire crossed her arms. "I'm not wearing those shoes, Katherine."

"Yes, you are." Kat unzipped the garment bag. "Because once you hit Ethan with the one-two punch of those shoes and this dress"—she pulled out a glossy black sheath—"he'll be putty in your hands. No. Scratch that." A wicked grin spread across her face. "When he's in your hands, he *won't* be putty. And that works perfectly with our mission statement. Do you wanna hear it?"

"No."

"Too bad." Kat displayed the shiny, seductively

sinful dress in her upturned palms and sauntered to where Claire stood rooted in the kitchen archway. "Our goal is for you to score with one of the nation's top goal scorers."

"Sheesh, Kat." Claire grimaced. What if my kids heard you say that?"

"Come on, give me a little credit. I know they're playing at Deb and Mike's house while you're on your date. I heard you're planning to pick them up by nine o'clock." Kat tsked and looked at her with a clear expression of pity. "It's a Saturday. You should enjoy the night with Ethan, not rush home after dinner."

"My kids have a bedtime, Kat. I'm not going to make them sit around late at night at Deb's house and wait for me to finish partying with my boyfriend."

"Of course not. That's why I'm going to pick them up from Deb's after you head out on your date. I'm staying with Ty and Grace here tonight so you don't have to worry about a curfew."

Claire's spine straightened. Even if well meant, it still grated on her nerves when anyone tried to control her life. "I didn't ask you to do that."

"Ethan did," Kat said, raising her hand to halt the protest forming on Claire's lips. "He also wanted me to pass along a message to you."

"What?" Claire asked, crossing her arms.

"He asked you to trust him."

The simple request deflated her anger in one long, slow exhale. Ethan deserved her trust, and she'd give it to him. "Okay."

Kat's eyebrows shot up. "I expected a bigger fight. I know how hard it is for you to relinquish control."

"I trust him."

"Glad to see maturity has vastly improved your taste in men," Kat said. "I never understood what you saw in Jackass."

"Even though I appreciate your undying loyalty, you should probably stop calling him Jackass. The divorce wasn't completely his fault. We should have never gotten married." Claire shrugged. "I was too young and naive then to know the difference between sex, romance, and love."

"And now you know?"

"Absolutely. Sex fuels the body, romance fuels the ego, and love fuels the soul."

"Holy shit." Kat's eyes went wide. "Romance fuels the ego? Bitter much?"

"Not bitter, I'm just tired of people confusing romance and love. Unlike love, romance doesn't last. Sure, it's nice when Ethan gives me flowers or compliments my appearance or plans a candlelit dinner. My ego enjoys the attention and the knowledge that he's attracted to me. But the resulting feelings of excitement and mystery, aka romance, shouldn't be the foundation of any relationship."

Braced for Kat's opinionated response, Claire stared her down. She'd meant what she'd said. No matter what Kat thought, Claire didn't feel bitter about it, only tired. Tired of bucking society. Tired of trying to stop romance from making any important decisions in her life.

Kat gave one curt nod. "I understand."

A jolt of surprise snapped Claire's head back. "You do?"

"Yeah. You don't trust picnic baskets, sunsets, or long walks along the shore. Got it. But we can still try to get you laid. Now go put on this dress."

"You're relentless," Claire groaned.

"I'm trying to return a favor. You once told me that I should enjoy the blinding-hot sex that comes at the beginning of a relationship and then get out before either of us were stupid enough to make it permanent."

"You ended up pregnant."

"I ended up with an amazing son and husband, but that's not the point." Kat shrugged a shoulder. "You encouraged me to have a little fun. Now I'm doing the same for you."

"Maybe we've already slept together."

"Oh, puh-lease." Kat rolled her eyes. "Ethan looks at you like a starving man eyes a side of beef. And you look at him the same damn way. Except I can tell you're trying to fight the desire rather than embrace it. You'd both look a hell of a lot more content if you were actually getting some."

Claire couldn't deny it. While her daily fantasies about having sex with Ethan tantalized and tempted, she'd fought those fantasies for fear of losing even more control of the unwieldy situation. But somewhere along the way, she might have lost control anyway.

"Even though she needs to finesse her delivery, I agree with Kat," Hannah said, unpacking a small bag of cosmetics.

"What do you think, sis?" Kat asked with a devilish grin, extending the dress to her. "Ready to change?"

And that was the real question, wasn't it?

Change. Was she finally ready to risk changing the life that had worked since her divorce?

"Listen to your sisters, pumpkin. Every woman deserves some fun in the boudoir."

Holy smokes, even Mrs. D thought she should go for it. "Fine," Claire huffed, throwing both hands into the air. Good chance she'd already given a big chunk of her heart to Ethan. How much more damage could she do by giving him her body as well? She snatched the dress from Kat. "But I'll never forgive you guys if I end up looking like an overdressed call girl." He'd already mistaken her for a hooker once; she didn't need to repeat the experience tonight.

Claire stomped to the half-bath off the hallway. She shouldn't have caved so easily. She wished she could say she wasn't interested in having sex with Ethan, but nobody would've bought such a ridiculous lie. Truth was, she wanted Ethan to see her as beautiful, sexy, and feminine. Right now, she couldn't resist the idea of him burning for her as much as she burned for him.

For better or worse, operation 'slutty makeover party' was a go.

She poured herself into the overtly sexual dress and contorted her arm to close the exposed zipper that ran the length of her spine. The dress ended just above her knees and hugged her tight enough both to render the small straps unnecessary as well as shove the swell of her breasts above the low-cut neckline.

She smoothed her hands down the slick fabric encasing her hips and tried to fight back nerves. She knew Ethan's time in Silver Bay was running out.

She'd repeatedly warned her kids that he'd be going back to soccer soon, even if he couldn't discuss the details of his return yet. A world-class athlete didn't walk away from a multi-million-dollar contract at the peak of his career to settle down with a small-town mom and her two kids.

"Okay, Cinderella," Kat said, banging on the bathroom door. "Are you ready for some smoking-hot makeup and a pair of slutty glass slippers?"

Claire groaned and thunked her palm against her forehead. In this getup she felt a hell of a lot more like Catwoman than Cinderella. Which was good, right? Catwoman would never confuse sex or romance with love.

Maybe Claire could compartmentalize sex for one night of her life, like Kat suggested?

Her core tightened. One sizzling night together might be enough to burn off the excessive amount of sexual tension between them. Or the sex might be mediocre, which would be both a bummer and a blessing.

Once, in college, she'd found an amazing pair of jeans in a high-end boutique. Way out of her budget, she'd left the shop without trying them on. For the entire next week, thoughts of those great jeans had kept sneaking into her mind. She'd returned to the boutique the following weekend in hopes of finding them on the discount rack. When the saleslady had seen her drooling over them, she'd encouraged Claire to try them on. "See if they fit. It'll be easier to let them go if they don't." Claire hadn't even gotten the jeans to her hips before she'd known they were wrong for her. She'd stripped them off and returned them to the saleswoman with a relieved smile.

"Trying Ethan on" tonight might result in a similar disappointment for both of them. Since reality-sex never lived up to fantasy-sex, odds were high she'd feel let down afterward. A dose of reality might be just what she needed. She could put their pretend dating and her all-consuming attraction to him behind her, and then they could move forward as friends.

Encouraged by the thought, she swung the bathroom door open.

Kat stood a foot away, two sexy black shoes dangling from the fingertips of her right hand. "Looking good, sis. Ready for your sure-to-get-laid *pièce de résistance*?" She waggled her eyebrows.

"I'm impressed." Claire sighed, lifting the shoes from Kat's hands. "It takes talent to make the most beautiful language in the world sound dirty." She propped a hand on the door jamb for balance and leaned over to slip on the heels.

"I have the ability to make just about anything sound dirty." With a look of feigned modesty, Kat brushed a few dark strands of hair from her face with her pinky. "It's a gift," she purred. Then she grabbed Claire's hand and yanked her toward the kitchen. "Now come on. We have less than forty-five minutes to fix your hair and makeup."

"What's wrong with my hair and makeup?"

"Nothing if you want to sell a bunch of cabinets and furniture," Kat responded dryly. "Hannah's job is to give you a look more fitting for a bedroom than a boardroom. Sit." Kat pointed her finger at the barstool next to Hannah's makeup station.

Claire obeyed Kat's bossy command and sank down.

"I've got one more thing to take care of while Hannah works her magic. Back in a jiff." Motioning for Deb to follow her, Kat strode from the room.

Claire eyed the empty doorway with a feeling of wary unease. "I should probably try to stop her from doing whatever she's about to do."

"What's the point?" Hannah dusted a light shimmer of powder onto Claire's face. "She'll do it anyway. She's tenacious." A slight smile softened her words. "The only reason I'm here is because she told me there was a family emergency. By the time I realized her idea of an emergency was getting you laid, we were halfway to your house. Besides, once I heard Mrs. D's mission statement, I figured this would be way more entertaining than working on a new cheesecake recipe."

"Mrs. D came up with the mission statement?" Claire whisper-hissed with a sideways look at the elderly church organist.

"Oh yeah." Hannah gave a slow, wide-eyed head nod. "Apparently, Kat was helping out at Mrs. D's house when she got the phone call about your date. They decided you needed help, and well," she said with a shrug, "here we are."

"Lucky me," Claire mumbled.

A half hour later, Claire took in her reflection in the entryway mirror and gulped. Hannah had played up the slight slant of Claire's eyes with black liner, a smoky shadow, and heavy mascara. Next, she'd curled, tousled, and sprayed Claire's hair into a sexy, bouncy style that fell about her shoulders in artful disarray. Paired with the sleek dress and five-inch heels, the entire look screamed sex. Loudly.

"You're sure it's not too much?" she asked,

shifting her gaze to the reflections of the four overly pleased-looking ladies standing behind her.

They shook their heads in unison.

"You're sure he's going to like it?"

Four heads nodded confirmation.

"And you're sure I don't look like a call girl?"

Mrs. D squinted, considering the question. "Maybe a little bit, pumpkin. But not one who works a corner or anything. You look like one of those classy escorts. You know, the ones that make the big bucks," she said with a thumbs-up and an encouraging smile.

Panic dropped her belly. "I'm going to change back."

"No, you're not." Kat turned her from the mirror. "I know you try to play down your sexuality, so playing it up for once is uncomfortable. Don't worry. You look amazing." Kat stepped around Claire and pulled a small suitcase from the hall closet. "To go along with his surprise. Ethan asked me to pack you an overnight bag."

"Overnight?" Claire heard the high-pitched squeak of shock in her voice. She took a deep breath and tried again. "Did he say where we were going to be spending the night?"

"Didn't ask." Kat shrugged.

The doorbell rang.

"Looks like Ethan's a couple of minutes early." Kat glanced at the time on her phone screen, a wicked grin curving her lips upward. "He must be anxious to see you. Come on, ladies, let's leave through the back door." She pointed toward the kitchen. "By the way, big sis, I packed a few new risqué garments to enjoy on your trip with Ethan."

She clicked her tongue and winked. "You're welcome."

Claire took a calming breath and waited to hear the backdoor click closed behind her dubious makeover crew. Before she had time to overthink the situation, she swung the front door open.

Ethan stood on her doorstep wearing a perfectly tailored dark suit, a pressed light-gray button-down, a sleek silver tie, and the megawatt smile that turned her insides to liquid. His brilliant-blue eyes flashed with surprise, then darkened with palpable desire as he scanned her body.

His gaze lingered when he reached her toes. "Nice shoes," he murmured.

Her heart pounded in her chest, and her breathing quickened. His low, husky voice electrified her nerve endings and shot off a wave of lust so intense she had to fight back the urge to physically throw herself on top of him.

She licked her suddenly dry lips. "I thought you'd like them."

He returned his gaze to hers. "What I'm feeling right now is a hell of a lot stronger than like." He lifted the suitcase by her side and offered her his arm. "Ready?"

Claire slipped her arm through his. "Absolutely."

THIRTEEN

ETHAN pulled the full-sized SUV he'd bought that morning to a stop at the small executive airport outside of Silver Bay. Claire glanced sideways at him in unspoken question. He gave her a reassuring smile. "You'll know where we're going soon. Promise."

"I hate surprises," she said with an adorable sigh of frustration.

He grinned and climbed from the car to retrieve their overnight bags from the back. He knew surprises were tough for her. The fact that she'd gone along willingly so far was a major sign of trust on her part. Hopefully, she'd be agreeable to everything else he proposed this weekend.

With the auction only a week away, tonight was technically their final date, and he intended to do whatever it took to keep her in his life.

His body tightened in appreciation as he helped her step from the car. Claire was a beautiful woman no matter what she wore. But tonight, she looked like every man's fantasy—a beautiful woman dressed to seduce to him.

He gritted his teeth and fought back the rush of desire. After his promise not to use romance as a seduction strategy, he'd kept his hands to himself—for the most part. But he didn't know how much control he had left. He wanted her more than he'd ever wanted anything or anyone in his life.

He drew in a breath and forced a tight smile. He had to stay focused on the goal. He needed Claire in more than his bed—he needed her in his future.

Shading her eyes from the sun, she peered at the small private jet waiting on the tarmac. She shook her head, then turned toward him with a playful smile and an amused expression lighting her beautiful eyes. "I'm not sure what I'm more surprised by, your new car, the plane, or the fact that you asked Kat to pack for me. I'm literally frightened to see what she put in there."

"Adds to the mystery and excitement, don't you think?"

She chuckled. "The last two months with you have provided more than enough excitement. I'm not sure I can survive more."

Unless Kat had managed to pack a herd of wildebeest in her suitcase, the surprise Ethan had planned for Claire would be a hell of a lot more exciting than anything coming out of that bag. Which would make Claire happy. Right?

An uncharacteristic nervousness tightened his gut. He was taking a major risk this weekend. Moving too quickly could scare Claire away.

Trying to shake off the doubt Logan had planted in his head, Ethan climbed the short set of stairs leading into the small jet. They exchanged greetings with the pilot and copilot. Apparently, Claire already knew the gray-templed, round-bellied Captain Chris Something-or-other, who'd flown her and her father on work trips before. Captain Chris reported on the weather and the expected flight time.

Ethan did a solid job faking his attention, nodding when expected and thanking the captain for the information, but the dude could have told him they were anticipating strong crosswinds and a flock of flying ferrets for all he heard.

"You look stressed. Afraid of flying?" Claire asked, lowering herself into one of the luxury leather seats.

Forcing a smile that hopefully looked more at ease than it felt, Ethan sat beside her. "If I say yes, would you hold my hand for comfort?"

Her lips twitched. She reached over the armrest and slipped her hand into his. Heat shot up his arm and quickly headed south. *Oh shit.* Getting hard over holding hands would ruin the romantic evening he wanted to give her.

He clenched his jaw. He had to relax. Too bad forcing relaxation was an idiotic endeavor that only ended up making him more tense.

In less than ten minutes, they were in the air. Not trusting his ability to keep the conversation romantic rather than sexual, Ethan sat eyes-front, rigid and silent.

Claire squeezed his hand gently and waited for him to look at her. "You're so tense. Anything I can do to help you unwind?" she asked with a flirtatious smile.

Ethan's heart stopped. A moment later it hammered back to life, thumping against his rib cage. Images of Claire helping him "unwind" played through his head. He wanted to explore her with his eyes, his hands, his mouth. He ached to sink into her, to feel her slick, tight heat wrapped around him as he moved inside of her.

Pull it together, DuBois. No way Claire was offering that fantasy.

He forced deep breaths into his lungs in a futile attempt to ignore the way her dress hugged her breasts and revealed a silky expanse of thigh. That seductive, barely-there scrap of fabric had Kat's name written all over it. Logan had been right; like a mouse asking a cat for help, Ethan had been a fool to involve her.

"I'm good." The hoarse words scraped across his dry lips. He swallowed and tried again, fighting to sound natural. "Just thinking about Kat." *Shit.* Ethan grimaced. "I mean—"

"Daydreaming about my little sister?" Claire arched a brow. "For a striker renowned for his finesse, Lucky, that move sure isn't going to help you score." She pinned him with narrowed eyes.

"I wasn't daydreaming about Kat." He kneaded the back of his neck with brutal force. "I was actually cursing my stupidity for involving her. I'm trying to be romantic here, Claire. But I'm about to break. Every cell in my body is screaming at me to rip everything—expect for those damn shoes—off of you and take you against the wall in the frigging bathroom."

Surprise flashed through her eyes.

"Shit," he mumbled with another grimace. "And that's the least romantic thing I've ever said to a woman."

A throaty laugh rumbled through Claire. She had the sexiest damn laugh. The first time he'd heard it at Bayside, he knew he had to have her. Hearing it now, he knew he had to keep her.

"I told you. I don't trust romance. It's not real. This ... " She ran a finger down his jawline and across his lips, leaving a trail of sparks in her wake. "This chemistry between us is real. Let's focus on that tonight and forget about the all-things-romantic checklist you've been working your way down."

"That obvious?"

"Did you look up how to be romantic on YouTube?" she asked gently, her expression suggesting she felt embarrassed for him.

He blew out a resigned breath. "It was wikiHow," he grumbled, wondering if he needed to strangle Logan. "What gave me away?"

"*Dirty Dancing.*"

"Really?" He went palms up. "I thought women loved that movie."

She laughed again and patted his thigh. "I appreciate the effort you've made to romance me, but I'd like to experience something real ... " She unclipped her seatbelt, stood to face him, and then extended her hand. "With you." She gave a hesitant smile and nodded to the back of the plane. "Ever gotten lucky on an airplane, Lucky?"

His gaze dropped to her breasts. He forced it to meet hers again, which should have helped, but seeing the desire dancing in her beautiful blue-green eyes only made him want her more. A low moan of desire escaped him. Unmoving and rigid, he stared into her eyes, desperate to read her mind. Was she offering this because she loved him, wanted him, or both? Would sex now hurt his chance at a future with her? And even if it would, was he truly strong enough to resist? Shit. He couldn't afford to mess this up.

Her smile fell as she dropped her hand back to her side. "Ethan, please say something." Her pale skin flushed red. "Your silence is really starting to freak me out."

He fisted his hands to stop himself from reaching for her. "You sure this is what you want?" His voice sounded exactly how he felt—raw, on edge, desperate. He held her gaze, every nerve in his body taut and strained and waiting for her response.

"Yeah," she murmured in a low, sultry tone, sending another surge of blood to his groin. "I want this. I want you more than I've ever wanted any other man."

The heat in her gaze burned through the last of his doubt. Who the hell was he to question what the lady wanted?

He slowly rose to his feet, stepped close enough to see the pulse beating in her neck, and took her hips in his hands. He gently pulled her to him. With the added height from those sexy heels, their bodies lined up perfectly. He didn't bother to hide his arousal, needing Claire to know her effect on him.

Her breath caught and her eyes flashed. With a sigh of pleasure, she slipped her arms around his neck.

Ethan brushed his lips against hers. She was soft and warm and intoxicating. He deepened the kiss, slipping inside her mouth to stroke and tease her with his tongue.

He'd intended to take his time and build the kiss from slow and thorough to passionate. But he'd underestimated Claire's response. With near violent intensity, she returned his kiss and ground her hips against him, escalating the kiss to scorching in a matter of seconds.

He pulled her tighter. Needing to explore more of her, he slid his hand into her hair and tipped her head to the side. He kissed his way from her mouth to her neck, licking and tasting the warm expanse of skin, unable to get enough of her.

Claire squirmed in his arms and grabbed the lapel of his suit jacket. "Off," she commanded, shoving the jacket backward.

He released his grip on her long enough to shake out of the coat, yank off his tie, and toss them both on one of the ten empty airplane seats. He pulled her back to him and returned his attention to her neck, collarbone, and the soft, exposed swell of her breasts. Every taste of her stole a little more of his control. He needed to sink into her soon or he'd lose his mind.

Thank God, there was no flight attendant. They were alone except for the captain and copilot behind a door at the front of the plane.

He cupped one breast and ran his thumb across the silky fabric covering her nipple. Letting out a gratifying purr-like noise, Claire dropped her head back and ground her hips against the rigid length of him. Loving her response, he flicked his thumb across her nipple again before giving the same attention to her other perfect breast.

"I need to touch you," she panted, yanking his shirt out of the waistband of his pants and fumbling to undo the buttons. Her unsteady fingers were unable to finish the job. "Screw it." She grabbed his shirt and ripped it open, launching the last two buttons across the aisle. She shoved his shirt wide and stared at him. "Finally," she murmured, running her hands up his abs and across his chest.

Now. He had to have her now. He slid his hands to her ass and lifted her to straddle his waist. "Come on. I can't wait another damn minute to peel that dress off of your beautiful body, and I don't want to get caught bare-assed in the seats."

With another sultry-sounding laugh, she wrapped her legs around his waist and clung to his shoulders as he maneuvered them down the narrow aisle. "You give a whole new meaning to in-flight service."

He chuckled, boosted her higher to support her with one arm, and then slowly lowered the long zipper running the length of her dress with his free hand. "I aim to please."

Claire threaded her fingers through his hair and tugged, positioning his mouth inches from hers. "Me too." She dropped her mouth to his in a fiery kiss that rocketed a fierce bolt of desire straight to his groin.

Which totally screwed with his finesse. But even though he bumped into a few seats along the way, he managed to get them to the back of the plane in record-breaking time.

"That was a wild ride, cowboy." Claire grinned down at him as they jolted to a stop against the back wall.

"Sorry." He nuzzled her neck and squeezed her ass. "My equilibrium is off. Too much blood flowing south."

Laughter bubbled through her. "You could have blamed it on turbulence."

"Damn. Good point." He nipped her neck, making her squirm in response. "Can I change my answer?"

"Nope, but you can make it up to me by being just as wild on the other side of the bathroom door." She giggled and buried her head in the crook of his neck. "I never thought those words would come out of my mouth. Ever. We really have kicked romance to the curb, haven't we?"

"Whatever makes you happy," he murmured against her soft skin.

With Claire still wrapped tightly around him, they stumbled, half-undressed and laughing, through the bathroom door. Ethan's blood hummed with a mixture of lust, elation, and love. He'd never been happier in his life. And in the sound of Claire's throaty laughter and the look in her expressive eyes, he could tell she felt the same.

Tonight, he couldn't lose.

FOURTEEN

CLAIRE slid from his arms and ran her gaze up and down the gorgeous man in front of her. His chest heaved, his breathing as ragged as hers. Even though the edges of her vision blurred, Ethan remained perfectly in focus.

She watched him kick the bathroom door shut behind them, the movement emphasizing the contours of his abs. Desire flowed through her, pooling in a pulsing ache between her thighs. Suddenly, her dress felt too tight around her swollen breasts. She slipped off the straps and shimmied until the fabric slid down her body, pooling in a glossy circle at her feet.

Ethan groaned as he did a slow scan down her. His gaze lingered on her naked breasts, lacy black panties, and of course, her notorious shoes. "You're perfect," he murmured, stripping off his shirt.

He wrapped an arm around her waist and hauled her into him until she was flush against his erection. She gasped in pleasure and arched her back to increase the pressure on her pulsing core. Ethan took advantage of the position and licked, sucked, and nipped at her breasts. He teased the swollen flesh, circling her nipples but never touching. She thrashed in his arms, trying to maneuver, coax, and eventually beg him to take her into his mouth.

Beyond desperate, she resorted to threats. "Ethan, I swear, if you keep toying with me, I'll make you pay." *Damn*. Rather than stern, her voice sounded breathless and wanton.

"That sounds more like a reward than a punishment."

"It won't feel like one. I'll make you just as desperate and out-of-control as I feel."

"Looking forward to it." He slid aside the wisp of fabric between her legs and sucked her aching nipple into his mouth.

Claire's every nerve was focused on what he was doing to her. "Please, Ethan." She squirmed against him.

He traced her wetness with a finger and bit down softly on her nipple in his mouth. She clung to his shoulders, spread her legs as far as the space allowed, and leaned back even more, desperate to give him complete access.

His fingers finally found her sensitive apex. Slowly, oh so slowly, he circled her once, twice. Already she was shaking on the edge of release. When his hand left her heated center, she whimpered in frustration.

"It's okay, honey. I won't leave you like this," he murmured.

Shifting breasts, he sucked her other peak into his mouth and slipped two fingers inside her. She cried out and rocked against his hand. He pulled out and pushed into her again, finding and circling her tight bundle of nerves with his thumb.

Claire threw her head back and screamed his

name as she shook in mindless release. Clinging to his shoulders, she gasped for breath as wave after wave of pleasure rolled through her.

Slipping his fingers from her, Ethan looked at her with a mixed expression of pleasure and pride. "That was the sexiest damn thing I've ever seen," he growled.

A bump of turbulence shook the floor. Claire felt the plane turn to the right, and Ethan gripped her hips to steady her. Her body tightened again. The first taste of pleasure had only made her crave him more.

Damn it, she needed to accomplish that not-so-ridiculous-anymore mission statement. She needed to score with him. Right now. She eyed the luxury bathroom with a scowl. While pristine and spacious by commercial plane standards, it still wasn't large enough for them to maneuver easily. How were they supposed to manage sex?

"Claire, honey, I'm sorry. I should have never … not in here. Not like this." Ethan gently tipped her chin up to face him. Regret etched his taut expression.

"Huh?" she asked, distracted.

"You look upset. I'm sorry—"

"Ethan," she interrupted, waving off his concern, "stop apologizing for the best orgasm of my life and help me figure out a way for us to have sex in here."

She turned her back to him, assessing the sink. They couldn't stop now. She still hadn't "tried him on," so to speak. Maybe she could balance on the narrow countertop …

She heard the metallic clank of Ethan unbuckling

his belt and the sound of his zipper lowering. She met his heated gaze in the mirror. Her spirits lifted even more when he placed a condom on the countertop beside them. A husky laugh slipped from her throat.

"Did you come up with a game plan?" she asked, stepping from the panties he'd peeled off of her from behind.

Watching her in the mirror, Ethan reached one arm around her to toy with her breasts and slid the other hand across her belly, heading lower. "I'm a true believer that you can accomplish anything if you want it badly enough." He kissed and suckled her neck while his fingers toyed, teased, and tormented her.

He continued the exquisite torture until she was panting and thrashing in his arms. Unable to take any more, Claire reached back and wrapped her hand around his impressive erection.

Ethan gasped and tensed behind her. "Claire," he said in warning.

With a surge of feminine power, she stroked the length of him and circled her thumb over his slick end. "Yes?" she asked in an innocent tone, studying his reaction in the mirror.

"If you keep doing that"—he broke off, groaning as she did it again—"this is going to be over sooner than either of us wants."

She spun in his arms, facing him at last. "The sooner we finish, the sooner we can start again." She reached for the condom. "Time to see if you fit," she whispered to herself, her words barely louder than a thought.

He stilled. "Honey, I'm not a small guy." He

shook his head, looking equally confused and concerned. "But I've never had a problem fitting before."

"Sorry." She fought a laugh. "Metaphor."

"Do I wanna know?"

"Nope." She handed him the condom.

He studied her for a breathless moment, then made quick work of rolling on the condom. He boosted her up to straddle his waist again, only this time, they were skin to skin. With the tip of his warm, hard erection positioned directly between her thighs, Ethan turned them around and maneuvered until her back rested pressed against the door.

She clung to his shoulders, propped one slutty shoe on the tiny countertop and braced the other one against the wall. She arched her back and squirmed, desperate to feel him inside her. Ethan cupped her bottom to hold her steady. He rotated his hips, spreading her slickness, and moved forward inch by inch in the most frustratingly slow pace in the entire flipping world.

Done waiting, Claire slammed her hips into him, burying him to her core. She cried out in pleasure as her body stretched to accommodate his size.

Ethan swore but didn't pull away. Instead, he gripped her hips and held her flush to his groin. Claire wiggled and shifted, craving friction, pressure, release.

He began rotating his hips, stimulating the nerve endings deep inside her in a rhythm designed to drive her out of her mind. Circling inside, pulling completely out, thrusting back in … Each shift in movement brought her closer to the edge. She whimpered from the denied gratification.

Finally, his control snapped. With a ragged oath, he thrust in and out of her with a building, blinding speed. She threw her head back, fought to spread her legs wider, and arched against him. Every muscle in her body tensed, craving blissful release. He drove into her over and over, slamming her back into the door.

She screamed out and fell over the edge. Spasming around him, her muscles clutched to keep him inside her every time he slid from her before thrusting back in.

As she rode the waves of pleasure back to earth, Ethan tensed, cried out her name, and slammed into her one final time.

Still holding her to him, he leaned forward to rest his forehead next to her against the door. "I'm going to need you to travel with me from now on," he panted, catching his breath. "Never going to be satisfied with a movie and a bag of pretzels again."

Claire lowered her feet to the floor. Thankfully, even with wobbly legs and *F*-me shoes, she managed to support herself. "I'm sure you can get along without me." She patted his shoulder and moved to step by him with a teasing smile.

"Maybe I don't want to." His serious expression and grave voice surprised her.

The room instantly felt ten times smaller.

Claire gulped and tried to think of a way to lighten the pulsing intensity. "You might reconsider when you see what I did to your expensive shirt." She bent down, scooped up a pile of his clothes, and shoved them into his chest.

She retrieved her panties and dress, and with her back to him, she struggled to get redressed. She could feel Ethan dressing too. She bumped her shin on the toilet and her funny bone on the faucet, doing her best to avoid contact with him.

Swearing under her breath, she fought back her rising anxiety. What the hell had she done? Nothing like having mind-blowing sex in an airplane bathroom with a fake much-younger boyfriend who happened to be your son's soccer coach to really make you question the life decisions that had brought you to this point. She sucked in a breath and then another. She felt a major freak-out moment coming on.

Two warm hands gripped her shoulders. "Don't overthink this," Ethan soothed, turning her to face him.

"I'm not," she lied, rather poorly judging by his skeptical look.

"It may have lacked romance, but nothing that happened between us was wrong. No need to feel embarrassed."

"I ripped the buttons off your shirt!" Claire scrunched her eyes closed. "I was totally out of control." She bit her lip and pressed her fingertips to her temples.

"I know." He took her hands in his and lowered them from her face. "I loved it."

She made a face.

"And I also love that you're a strong, capable woman who has a grip on everything." He brushed each of her open palms with a soft kiss. "But anytime you wanna let go for a little while, I'll catch you."

Doing her damnedest not to hyperventilate, Claire studied the amazing man in front of her. She might have a few years on him in age, but she had nothing on him in maturity or strength of character.

Ethan's unique blend of patience and persistence was incredibly appealing. Whether a professional soccer player, a volunteer coach, or a pretend boyfriend, he was determined to do his best and dedicated himself fully to whatever job he undertook. He was kind, intelligent, funny, good to her kids, gorgeous and the perfect fit—metaphorically speaking—and rather than getting upset about her independent streak and control issues, he accepted who she was while also promising to be there for her if she ever cared to change.

Searing love pierced her heart and burned into her soul. Her fears were confirmed. She'd totally screwed up and had fallen completely in love with Ethan.

She sucked in a breath and blew it out. Her fingers turned numb, and her heart slammed against her chest.

Ethan gripped her hands, his expression instantly concerned. "What's wrong?"

She couldn't seem to stop shaking her head. "I'm an idiot. I knew from the beginning you were only in town temporarily. I warned my kids over and over again not to get too attached. 'Ethan's a great guy, but he'll be going back to his real life soon, so don't be upset when he leaves.' And what the hell did I do?" Her voice squeaked, her words racing as quickly as her heart. "I fell in love with a famous soccer star who can return to the excitement of professional sports and dating pop stars and active-wear models whenever he wants."

"I told you. I'm retired from soccer." His bright-blue eyes shone. He looked beyond pleased with himself. "I'm also retired from casual dating."

"ESPN reported your team doubled its offer for you to return."

He shrugged. "Doesn't mean I'm going to accept. I've actually been working on a plan to go to college. I've been accepted to a university in England. But now I'm thinking about applying to Marquette instead since I could commute there from Silver Bay. I'd like to get a teaching degree."

"You'd be a great teacher, but what about soccer?"

"I've made a hell of a lot of sacrifices for it over the years. The relationship with my mom, fun, friendships, and nearly every second of my free time as a kid. Hell, sometimes it felt like I didn't even have a childhood. After countless years of competitive play, my body aches, which I could ignore, but I've lost the hunger that used to drive me. And that I can't ignore." He blew out breath. "I've got little desire to go back now and compete against kids ten years younger than me and looking to prove themselves." A crooked smile lifted the corner of his sexy mouth. "I told you. I've set my sights on a new goal. A better goal." He traced his thumb down her jawline and across her bottom lip.

Heat crept up her neck and a nervous giggle slipped out. "Think you already scored that goal."

"Not quite." Reaching into his pocket, Ethan pulled out a tiny velvet bag. "I'd planned a candlelit dinner, sunset walk, and even a few French love songs leading up to this, but considering your continued distrust of romance, I can't think of a better place to ask you to spend your life with me than an airplane bathroom."

Claire gasped, stunned. Thoughts careened in her head, making it impossible to think straight, let alone form actual words.

Ethan slipped a silver ring with an enormous emerald-cut diamond from inside the bag.

Her heart stopped, then pounded back into action.

"I love you, Claire. I love your strength and warmth, your intelligence and independence. I love that you're an amazing mom, patient sister, and caring friend who's willing to help fix any problem. I love that when I'm with you, you make me so damn happy that I spend my days thinking of ways to make you happy too." He paused and swallowed hard. "I didn't even know anything was missing until I met you. Now, I can't go back to my old life. It's not enough anymore. I want to be with you. I need to be with you." He took a shaky breath that ended in a hopeful smile. "Marry me, Claire." He extended the sparkly ring toward her. "I need you by my side now and forever."

Her pulse beat wildly in her neck, and the white noise of rushing blood filled her ears. She had to say something but didn't know what to say. What could she say? What *should* she say? She watched his smile slip and the corners of his eyes tighten and knew her silence was freaking him out. It was freaking her out too. She had to say something!

"Change," she forced out before the thick lump of emotion in her throat suffocated the rest of her words.

He blinked.

She cringed.

God, she hated surprises.

FIFTEEN

ETHAN tilted his head to the side and studied her, his eyebrows squished together in confusion. "Honey, I'll change whatever you want. The ring, this rumpled shirt, my hair color—anything, just name it."

Claire's giggle held a tinge of hysteria. "Sorry. I didn't mean that you needed to change. You're wonderful and so is your hair. And for what it's worth, I'll always have a special place in my heart for this rumpled, button-missing shirt." She placed her palm over his heart and smoothed a wrinkle.

She drew in a breath. "Change used to be easy for me. I willingly embraced it, naively assuming I could have, be, do anything I wanted in life. That's why I married Jack so quickly. My romantic heart jumped"—she cringed—"no, it dived into the promise of happily ever after. But I learned change isn't always progress. Sometimes it's better, safer, to *not* change. After my marriage failed, I didn't trust my judgment."

Her voice cracked, and she swallowed hard at the pressure in her throat. "I didn't trust *myself* to make any life-changing decisions for fear of messing everything up again. So even though every single person in town seemed to think I needed to find a new man, I feared letting one close might be a mistake and ruin the happy life my kids and I have together."

Ethan's brow creased in concern. "I love Ty and Grace too. I swear to you, I won't do anything to—"

"I know." She stopped him. "You're kind and generous. You're dedicated and determined. You ask for my opinion and respect my answers. You're positive, supportive, and patient. Plus, you make me laugh and you accept my quirks. You're the perfect guy for me. I know it in my heart and in my head. Though I swore I'd never get swept away in another whirlwind romance, I can't help it. We're perfect together, and I'd be a complete idiot to let you go." The rightness of her words sent a rush of love through her, steadying her voice and her resolve.

Ethan's heart hammered beneath her hand. "Claire, honey, I've lost too many games in the last few minutes of a match to celebrate before the final whistle. Please, tell me that's a yes."

Emotion flooded her heart with joy and her eyes with tears as an irrepressible smile bloomed across her face.

"Yes."

The next few moments passed in a blur of straightening clothes, laughter, and kisses. Eventually, Ethan slipped the ring on her finger, took her hand, and led her from the bathroom. She floated down the aisle behind him in a surreal, giddy bubble of love and hope.

Then Ethan came to an abrupt halt. "Is something wrong?" He directed the question toward the front of the plane, not at her.

The copilot stood outside the cockpit, looking both serious and uncomfortable. "Sorry, folks. I need you to take your seats."

The sharp edge of concern in his voice popped her stupid bubble of giddiness.

Ethan glanced at his watch. "We haven't been in the air long enough to have arrived already."

"We've turned around and are preparing to land in Silver Bay. Captain received a message from Ms. Bennett's father." He looked at Claire, sympathy filling his eyes. "I'm sorry, ma'am. There's been an accident."

•••

Shortly after earning the dubious title of world's most unromantic proposer, Ethan parked in front of the emergency room, hit the flashers, and hustled to keep up with Claire as she ran past an old guy in a wheelchair and bolted through the automatic doors.

She'd been on the phone with Kat since the moment they landed. From the one-sided conversation, he'd learned Grace had dislocated her elbow after falling off the trampoline. But it sounded like the bigger concern was a possible head injury.

"Mom!" The first to spot Claire, Ty raced across the waiting room and flew into her outstretched arms.

Hanging back, Ethan watched Claire's petite, polished mom, Ann, and her large, slightly intimidating dad, Richard, stand up from the chairs in the corner of the room. Kat, Jack, and Gemma rose beside them. The group made their way toward where Claire stood near the entrance. While they all shared the same look of concern, he took the fact that there were no tears of distress as a good sign.

"It was horrible, Mom," Ty said, hugging Claire like he never planned to let go. "Grace fell off the trampoline trying to do a flip. I tried to help her, but her arm was bent at a really weird angle and she was crying and screaming. I'm so sorry. I know you said we shouldn't do flips."

"It's okay." Claire kissed the top of Ty's head, then stroked his hair in a soothing motion while she held him close. "I'm not mad. I'm just worried." She shifted her gaze to the group gathered around them. "How is she?"

Their combined expressions shifted from anxious to astonished when they saw the ring on her finger.

"Oh my God!" Gemma blurted out. "Did you—"

"Her scan showed she didn't suffer a head injury so that's a major relief," Jack interrupted, giving Gemma a warning look meant to keep her quiet.

Kat stepped forward. "But they had to take her into surgery because they weren't able get her elbow back in without sedation."

"We could hear her screaming all the way out here while they tried to put it back in place." Ty's frightened, tear-filled voice sounded muffled he was pressed so tightly to Claire. "She kept screaming for you. But you weren't here."

A hard knot of guilt landed heavy in Ethan's gut. If he hadn't planned the secret trip, Claire would have been by Grace's side.

The blood drained from Claire's face. She drew in a shaky breath as tears slid down her pale cheeks.

"I know how scary this is, and I'm so sorry I wasn't here for you and Grace. But I'm here now, and I'm not going anywhere. Everything is going to be okay. I promise." She kissed his head again. "Grandma, Grandpa, and Aunt Kat look like they could use a cup of coffee. Would you take them to the cafeteria while we wait for Grace to come out of surgery?"

He sniffled. "Could I get a lemonade?"

Claire gently pulled away and smiled down at Ty. "Sure, kiddo. I love you."

Ty wiped the back of his hand across his nose. "Love you too." He stepped back and spotted Ethan. "Hey, Ethan." He gave him a watery smile, obviously feeling better after a big hug from his mom.

"Hey, champ." Ethan stepped forward to ruffle the boy's blond hair. "Good job helping take care of your sister."

Ty beamed. "Thanks." He shifted his eyes from Ethan to Claire and made a face. "Why are you guys dressed so funny?" He pointed to Ethan's chest. "And why is your shirt missing buttons?"

Ethan froze. Claire sucked in air. Gemma giggled. Jack and Richard snorted. Thankfully, Ann stepped forward and took her grandson's hand in hers. "They are dressed up for a fancy date. I imagine you'll wear nice clothes to impress a lady someday too." She steered Ty toward a long hallway leading from the emergency room. "Let's go get that lemonade."

"What about the buttons?" Ty asked, looking over his shoulder with a crinkled brow.

"Oh, those probably fell off by accident." Ann wrapped her arm around his shoulders and continued down the hall.

"Wait for me," Richard called. "I'll be damned if I'll listen to how those buttons actually came off," he muttered, hurrying after his wife.

"I'm so sorry, sis." Kat wrapped her arms around Claire and pulled her close. "I went inside to start dinner. I didn't know she would try to do a flip."

"It's not your fault," Claire said, hugging her back. "I was caught off guard when you told me you were watching the kids and forgot to go over the trampoline rules. I'm just grateful you took care of her when she fell and were able to get Mom, Dad, Jack, and Gemma here so quickly. Thankfully, you guys were here for Grace." Claire pulled back to look Kat in the eye. "One more favor?"

"Of course."

"Could you go to the cafeteria and help keep Ty's mind off the surgery? I need to take care of something before I join you guys there."

Kat studied Claire for a moment. Even from a few feet away Ethan could see the younger woman's eyes tighten with worry. "Claire, don't—"

"Please," Claire interrupted quietly.

Kat drew in a slow breath then turned her gaze to Ethan. She seemed to be sending him a silent message, but before he could figure out what the hell Kat was trying to tell him, she turned back to Claire. "Okay," she said on a resigned sigh before starting down the long corridor to find her parents and nephew.

"We'll go too." Jack took his wife's hand and pulled her toward the departing group.

"No way. I wanna hear about that ring." Gemma grabbed Claire's left hand and pulled it close for inspection. "OMG. It's huge. How did he propose? Was it super romantic?"

Claire pulled her hand back and gave Gemma a tight-lipped head shake.

"Oh, I'm so stupid." Gemma's eyes widened. "You don't want to talk about that now. I totally get it. But try not to worry about Grace. I just know she's going to be fine. She's super strong, like you. You've done such an awesome job raising her." Gemma's eyes went from round to teary in less than a second. "I hope I can be as good as mom as you someday." Her words broke, and her face crumpled. "Sorry." She sniffed and rubbed a hand over her stomach which seemed to be getting larger by the day. "These silly pregnancy hormones have me in tears at least once a day."

"Let's get you and the baby some food. The nurse said they'd call us as soon as Grace is out of surgery." Jack placed his hand on his wife's lower back and finally succeeded in budging her from her spot. Gemma wrapped an arm around Jack's waist and leaned her head on his shoulder as he led her away.

Ethan wondered if Claire would ever lean on him for support. God, he hoped so. Not only did he want to grow old with her, he wanted to be there for her through the tough times along the way. Good teammates were always there for each other, celebrating the highs and fighting through the lows together.

"Can we talk?"

The bleakness in Claire's voice pulled Ethan's thoughts to the here and now. "Of course," he said, following her back outside.

The brisk fall wind, slammed into them the moment they stepped through the door. Claire continued down the sidewalk and around an unsheltered corner.

"Here, take my coat. You must be freezing in that dress."

Claire finally stopped walking and turned to face him. Confusion clouded her features. She glanced around as if just noticing the crappy weather.

"No. I'm fine." She looked at him, regret etched on her face. She slid the ring from her finger and extended it toward him. "I'm sorry I accepted this. It was mistake, my mistake. I knew better, and I'm truly sorry that I'm hurting you now."

Desperation snaked through him, ruthlessly constricting his heart into a hard knot of fear. "Don't do this," he pleaded, needing to change her mind. He knew she was hurting, but he could help her through this if she would only let him. "I love you, Claire. And I love your kids. I told you, I want to build a future with you. I'll do anything to make this work. Just tell me what I need to do to prove that to you."

She shook her head, the painful resolve in her eyes nearly bringing him to his knees. "I'm sorry, Ethan. There's nothing to prove ... Nothing you can do to change my mind." She took another step away from him. "It's not another game you can win if you work hard enough. I'm so sorry. I really am. But it's not your choice to make."

"You love me," he argued.

"I do." Her voice cracked as she lifted her hand toward his chest.

For a moment, he thought she planned to lay her

palm over his heart. Then all emotion drained from her eyes, and her hand dropped away.

"Tonight's wakeup call shook me from the dream I've pretended was real since the day I met you. For a few blissful moments, I fooled myself into believing I could have it all—a great guy, amazing kids, and a job I love." She shook her head and sniffled. "But I know that's not possible—"

"Don't." He reached for her, but she jerked away from his touch. A fist to the gut would have hurt less. He balled his hands and dropped them uselessly to his side. "Don't make this decision."

"I have to," she whispered, tearing him apart. "After the divorce, I had this made." Claire touched the pendant around her neck. "Ty's thumbprint makes up one side of the heart and Grace's the other, and that's the way it has to be. They deserve my whole heart. But the more I give to you—the more I give us—the less I have for my kids. Instead of flying off on a romantic getaway, I should have been there for Grace today. I should have been protecting her, holding her hand, and promising her everything would be all right. She needed comfort and kisses." Claire's voice trembled and tears streamed down her face. "She needed a mom—needed me, and I let her down." She drew in a breath and straightened her shoulders. "I won't do it again."

Guilt, regret, and determination poured off her in near palpable waves. And he was responsible for all of it.

The realization hollowed him to the core.

He'd told Logan he wanted to make Claire happy. But he'd been an asshole, doing what made him happy and stupidly assuming that would make her happy too. Instead of listening to her repeated attempts to tell him she didn't want a man in her life, he'd selfishly messed with the good life she'd put together for her and her kids.

Stepping closer, Claire swallowed hard and wiped the tears from her face. She gently took his hand and placed the ring in his palm, then brushed a soft kiss against his cheek. "Goodbye, Ethan." Her whisper broke with emotion.

Truly and utterly defeated for the first time in his life, Ethan watched the woman he loved—the woman he wanted to spend his future with—turn her back and walk away. And there wasn't a damn thing he could do about it.

SIXTEEN

ETHAN heaved a deep sigh and knocked on the gleaming white door in front of him. Waiting for a response, he looked down the street of well-maintained homes and mature trees. The houses in this neighborhood were small in size and large on character.

While no two looked alike, they all looked loved. There were no overgrown yards or untended flowerbeds in sight. Many of the porches welcomed visitors with bench swings and planters of orange and yellow flowers by their front doors. The cool fall breeze carried the smell of bonfires, the squeak of swing sets, and the laughter of children from more than one backyard.

Small-town America at its best.

Ethan should have realized sooner why his mom loved her home so much. But he'd focused all of his attention on reaching his goal without bothering to consider what she wanted.

He sighed again. He'd been doing a lot of sighing and moping since Claire dumped his ass three days earlier. His instincts and his aching heart—hell, every cell in his body—screamed at him to fight for her. But Claire's words haunted him. It wasn't his choice to make. He'd learned a valuable, if shitty, lesson. No matter how good his intentions or how much he loved someone, he couldn't make her want the same thing he wanted.

He knocked again, thinking Claire would be proud of him for what he was about to do. Thanks to the lesson she'd taught him, he finally understood how to fix, or at least help, his relationship with his mom.

He heard footsteps inside. The door swung open a moment later.

"Hey, Mom."

His mom's eyes flashed with surprise, and a tentative smile lifted the corners of her mouth. "Ethan, it's nice of you to stop by. You're lucky you caught me. I usually have office hours for my students after my Tuesday class, but it seemed far too pretty of a day to sit around an office." She stepped aside and extended a hand to invite him in. "I was just preparing a cup of tea. Would you like one?"

Damn. Tea again. "How about a water instead?" he asked, already knowing her response.

"I'll make you a tea." She shut the front door, started walking down a short hallway, and motioned for him to follow her. "It's full of antioxidants and has been shown to prevent cancer and heart disease. Much better for you than those sugar-filled sport drinks you like to push."

"One," he grumbled, scrubbing a hand down his face. "I did one Gatorade commercial. And I turned down a very lucrative second offer after you made me personally responsible for our nation's sky-high obesity rate."

She turned to face him, head cocked. "You turned it down?"

"Yes."

"How much was it worth?" she asked, sounding stern rather than pleased.

"A lot." He ground his teeth. He'd tried to do the right thing; he shouldn't feel defensive.

She gave a curt nod and stepped into a large, open-concept space. At one end of the room, there was a white love seat, two green-and-white patterned arm chairs, and a leather ottoman topped with a white tray holding coasters and a few *National Geographic* magazines. Along the opposite wall of the room, a decent-sized television hung above the wooden mantle of a white brick fireplace.

Ethan wasn't surprised to see the love seat and chairs faced each other rather than the TV. His mom always arranged furniture for conversation or reading, not for watching television. Hell, the real surprise was that she even *owned* a TV.

The modern kitchen at the far side of the room was fresh and bright and gleamed with stainless appliances, white cabinets, and stone countertops. Wide planks of rich brown wood ran underneath everything, making the space feel warm and welcoming.

"You remodeled," he said, following her into the kitchen.

"Last year." His mom placed two cups and saucers on the countertop, added tea bags, and poured steaming water into both of them. "I hired most of the work out. I did paint the cabinets myself." She looked at them fondly. "I have to admit, I found the work satisfying. I'm considering painting my guest room sage or possibly teal." She handed him a cup and saucer. "Let's have a seat in the living room, and you can tell me why you're here. I doubt it's to discuss paint colors."

He waited for her to take a seat, then sat down in the armchair across from her. He placed the tea he had no intention of drinking on the tray between them and took a few deep breaths, looking around the cozy-sized home and its charming decor.

"I was wrong," he said, returning his gaze to hers. "I shouldn't have bought you a house you didn't want." He sighed. "Or need. I've called the realtor. It'll be on the market in less than a week."

She made face. "That's ridiculous. Why would you sell such a perfect house?"

He scrubbed another hand down his face and let out a dry, humorless laugh. "I can't win with you. Never could. Don't know why the hell I thought today would be any different."

"I'm your mother. Why would you believe you have to win anything with me?" She shook her head. "I've never understood this competitive nature of yours. I attribute that personality trait to your father."

"Guess you should have been more selective choosing the other half of my DNA. Maybe if you'd picked the guy from page eight of the catalogue instead, you could have had the perfect son."

"There's no need for melodramatics." She sipped her tea, looking unfazed by his jab. "The man I selected had many athletic as well as academic accolades. Combining those with my own achievements meant that I was well aware you were likely to be gifted." On a small exhale, she returned her tea to the saucer and studied him with a sad expression. "And you are."

Ethan ground his teeth. "But not in the way wanted. You've always been disappointed that you had a son with a great right foot, not a great mind." He hated but couldn't seem to hide the bitterness in his tone.

She cocked an eyebrow. "I've never been disappointed in your talents. The only thing I find disappointing is your steadfast refusal to nurture all of your gifts. By the age of four, your reading and mathematical abilities were that of a child double your age."

"I've always been a quick learner." He shrugged off the comment.

"True. It's a fact I attribute to your elevated intelligence. I had your IQ tested when you were younger. While below Einstein's level, it still qualified you as a genius and predicted high levels of academic achievement in your future. But rather than joining Mensa, you joined a professional soccer team."

His mom shook her head. "If a strong right foot, as you say, was the totality of your abilities, I'd be happy for you to have found a career showcasing that gift. But you could have excelled at any of the elite colleges that offered you scholarships. Instead, you turned them all down. I feared that choice would have horrible repercussions in your life after soccer." She looked at him with a sad, tight smile. "I've always believed you have more to offer the world than simply being a form of entertainment—no matter how entertaining your talent."

"I never wanted to be a doctor, engineer, scientist, lawyer or whatever it is you wanted me to do with my life," Ethan snapped. "I wanted to be part of a team and play the sport I loved. I'll never regret that decision. And how would you know about my entertaining talent?" Ethan asked. "It's been over ten years since you've come to one of my games."

A small shudder shook her body. "I can't stand listening to the asinine comments the spectators yell at you. Or when they moan in frustration if you miss a shot. As if any of them could handle the ball with a fraction of the grace, skill, and intelligence that you do. I prefer to watch you play on that monstrosity." She nodded to the large television over the fireplace. "I find its mute button invaluable during your matches."

Slack-jawed, Ethan stared at his mom. "I didn't know—" He broke off, shaking his head to clear his thoughts.

"That I watched every one of your games." She finished his sentence. "No matter how much I believe you should have gotten a college degree instead of—or at least before—you played professional soccer, you're still my son. As ridiculous as it may sound, watching you play makes my chest fill with pride and accomplishment." She laughed softly. "As if I had somehow contributed to your talent for the game." His mom cleared her throat and looked away, seeming embarrassed by her admission.

Ethan froze, not sure what to say or do or feel. He hadn't known she'd been watching him all these years. He sure as hell had never thought she'd be proud of him for playing a sport.

Still a bit shell-shocked, he watched his mom fumble with her tea cup and dart her gaze around the room. Her uncharacteristic sign of nerves touched his heart as much as her words had.

"Thanks, Mom. It means a lot to hear you say that." He gave her a teasing smile. "If you'd let me know sooner, we might've avoided this whole house fiasco."

She shifted her gaze back to his, understanding lighting her eyes. "You bought me that house as bribery."

"Not bribery," he said, idiotically trying to defend the idiotic decision to buy her a house she never wanted. "I thought you'd appreciate my career choice more if you were able to enjoy some of its benefits."

She chuckled, looking like she found him funny as hell. "Ethan, dear, that's bribery."

He blew out a sigh and shrugged. "Seemed like a good idea at the time."

"I'm sorry that I didn't express my feelings sooner," she said. "You had an entire world telling you how wonderful you were. I never thought you needed to hear it from me as well. Especially since I'm your mother. I'm engineered to believe you are the most talented, wonderful, creative player to ever take the field."

"Wow. You really are biased," he teased, reaching for his cup. He took a sip, momentarily forgetting what was inside. He grimaced at the taste of the lukewarm, watered down liquid. "I'll never get used to this stuff," he muttered, glowering into the cup.

"You should drink it. It's good for you. If you plan to return to the game at your age, you're going to need all the health benefits you can get."

Ethan stiffened. "Who said I'm returning?"

"Everyone. Are you?"

"I wasn't going to. I'd been making arrangements to stay in Silver Bay. But now …"

His mom tipped her head to the side, considering his words. "But now you want to leave?"

"I don't know. Maybe." He stood up and started pacing around the room. "Claire broke up with me. I can't imagine living here—seeing her and the kids around town every day—and not being with them." He shoved a hand through his hair and sighed. Again. "Going back to soccer is the easiest and fastest way to get Silver Bay out of my mind."

"It's true." His mom nodded in agreement. "It's easier to quit than to fight for what you want. But the easier path is rarely the best. You of all people should know that."

"She doesn't want me in her life," he snapped. "I proposed. She said no. End of story."

His mom rose from the couch and walked up to him. "I'm sorry to hear that," she said, placing her hand on his arm. "I like Claire, Ty, and Grace. I'd hoped they could become a significant part of your life after soccer." She took a deep breath and paused. "You've never enjoyed solitude. Do you remember begging me to have more children when you were a child?"

"I do." Ethan said. "I wanted brothers and sisters to play with."

"It's why I registered you for soccer in the first place." His mother sounded both resigned and slightly amused.

"How many times have you regretted that decision?"

"Not once." Her expression grew serious. "You thrived in a team setting. It's why I spent countless hours driving you to trainings and attending weekend-long tournaments. Not to mention the cost every year." She shook her head slowly. "But I couldn't ask you to give it up. It fulfilled you in a way I've never quite understood." She looked away. "I suppose it's one of our many differences."

The small break in her voice and the hint of moisture he'd seen gathering in her eyes wiped clean the last of his frustration. He'd only seen her cry one other time in his life. That night years ago when they'd fought over his decision to turn professional rather than attend college.

Pissed off and righteous as only an eighteen-year-old could be, he'd called her a control-freak who wanted to keep him from his dreams. Even worse, he'd accused her of never being there for him and never truly understanding him. Even though he later apologized, he could still hear the sound of her quiet sobs as he'd thrown his stuff in a bag and left.

And maybe his mom had never understood his love of soccer, but she'd supported it anyway. To a cocky, barely-turned adult, her demand that he say no to a chance to play in the MLS seemed ludicrous. Now, a bit older, he could see she'd only been trying to help him secure a good future, not hold him back.

"We have some differences," he said quietly, waiting to say more until she met his eyes again. "We also have a lot in common. We're both stubborn, determined people who know what we want out of life and aren't afraid to work hard to make it happen."

"That's true." A hesitant smile curled her lips

upward. "Maybe I have played a small part in your soccer success after all?"

"Are you kidding?" He grinned down at her. "There's a part of you in everything I do."

Her expression softened, sending a wobble through her smile and a tear down one cheek.

"No tears." He wrapped his arms around her and pulled her against his chest for the first real hug they'd shared in years. "I promised myself I'd never make you cry again."

Resting her head against his shoulder, she hugged him back and sniffled. "I'm not crying. I'm just experiencing an overflow of positive emotions."

Ethan chuckled. "I believe 'happy tears' is the term you're looking for." He felt her smile against his shoulder, and for the first time since losing Claire, he didn't feel like complete shit. "I love you, Mom."

"I love you too," she said, eventually leaning back to study him with a long, hard look. "I can see you're hurting. I hate it."

"I love her."

"Give Claire time to change her mind. Most parents try to make decisions based off what they believe to be best for their children. But I can say from personal experience that we sometimes let fear or pride or past-experiences muck up those decisions. At least, reconsider putting the house on the market right away. It really is the perfect home—for you and Claire."

A vision of raising kids with Claire in the laughter and love-filled lakefront home flashed through his mind. Just as quickly, the knowledge that he'd never achieve that dream nearly brought him to his knees.

"When do you need to let your team know if you're accepting the offer?" she asked.

"By the end of the weekend." The thought of returning left him cold. The raging fire that used to fuel him to compete at the highest level had nearly extinguished. Hell, he'd felt it cooling for years. But one last push in the pros might be the perfect distraction for a brokenhearted dumbass like him.

"Are you going to leave Silver Bay?"

Shaking his head and wondering how the hell he'd gotten himself into this sorry state, Ethan clamped his eyes shut and pinched the bridge of his nose hard enough to bruise. "I think I have to."

"When?"

"Sunday morning." He'd rather put Silver Bay—or rather, his heartache—in his rearview mirror sooner, but he loved Claire too damn much to abandon her on Saturday night. "Are you going to the charity auction this weekend?" he asked.

"Of course. The entire town is talking about it. Will I see you there?"

With a wry smile, Ethan heaved another massive sigh. "I'll be hard to miss."

•••

Balancing a full glass of wine, a box of tissues, the remote, and a bag of assorted chocolates, Claire plunked down on her couch with no plan to get back up until she needed a refill. Or the bathroom.

It was the night of the infamous bachelor and bachelorette auction and she was beyond thankful to be sitting at home rather than hiding her pain from the town. Thankfully, her little sister had texted that morning to excuse Claire from the event. Too brokenhearted to care that it was an act of pity, Claire had gratefully accepted.

It had been a week since her engagement to and her disengagement from Ethan. A fresh wave of pain coursed through her at the memory. She closed her eyes and braced herself until it passed, or at least until the worst of it passed. The pain never fully left her. But it did lessen when she was with her kids or distracted at work. She hoped someday memories of her time with him would bring a faint smile to her lips instead of crushing her soul with the brutal knowledge of what could never be.

If only her stupid romantic heart would stop tricking her into thinking she could make a relationship work. First, she'd married Jack and thought they'd live happily-ever-after, and look how that turned out. Once he got to know her—really know her—Claire was fairly certain Jack didn't even like her that much.

Then she fell for Ethan and thought it was different because he saw and loved her for who she was in a way Jack never had. So she threw caution to the wind and gave him her heart, took his ring, and had the best sex of her life in an airplane bathroom. And what happened? She'd deserted her responsibilities and her children when they needed her the most.

At least no lasting harm had come to either kiddo. Grace came through the surgery with flying colors and had already snapped back to her happy, chatty ways. But the event still haunted Claire. It always would.

The old-fashioned buzz of her doorbell announced an unwelcome guest had arrived at her pity party for one. She cranked up the volume on the television and steadfastly ignored one, two, three more buzzes. Gritting her teeth and holding her breath, she waited in the silence following the last buzz, hoping like crazy the person had finally decided to—

Buzz.

"That's it," Claire grumbled, jumping from the couch and charging toward the door. Like a smoke detector alerting of a low battery, this annoyance was not going away until she took care of it. She assumed an expression of hardened disinterest and swung the door open, ready to tell whoever was ringing her bell to go the hell away—nicely of course.

Wearing a dark-red sweater dress, heeled, knee-high boots and an adorable baby bump, Gemma stood on her doorstep frantically waving for Claire to come out of the house. "Come on, we have to hurry. Jack thinks I'm in the bathroom."

"What are you doing here?"

"I came to take you to the auction."

"No way. I'm not leaving. The kids are sleeping over with friends, and I have a full bottle of chardonnay and *The Bridges of Madison County* on DVD. Thanks anyway." Claire slowly began to close the door. It didn't count as slamming it in Gemma's face if she did it slowly, right?

"Did you know Ethan took your place in the auction?" Gemma's perky voice drifted through the remaining two inches of open doorway a moment before it shut.

Wide-eyed in surprise, Claire swung the door

fully open. "He took my place?"

"Yep," Gemma said, stepping into the house and closing the door behind her. "Jack and I were talking to Kat a few minutes ago. She said Ethan offered to be in the auction instead of you. He made her promise not to tell you though." Gemma smirked. "But no one made me promise to keep my mouth shut, and I really thought you should know." She glanced at her phone. "We need to hurry. Ethan told Kat he's leaving town in the morning, so he's being auctioned off first so he can go on the date tonight with whoever buys him."

"He's leaving town?" Heart pounding, Claire's stomach dove at the thought. "Where is he going?"

"I don't know." Gemma shook her head. "You need to talk to him and figure all this out before it's too late. Come on." She held up her car keys. "I'll drive."

"I can't." She forced the words past the big lump of emotion in her throat.

Gemma wrinkled her nose in confusion. "Don't you love him?"

"Yeah," she whispered, her voice breaking over the word. "I love him, but I had to walk away."

"Why?"

Even though there were a couple of good reasons, Claire decided to share the one that was easiest and least embarrassing to justify. "Because I'm a mom, and my kids are my first priority. When I tried to add Ethan into my life, my kids ended up getting less of me in theirs."

"I thought Ty and Grace loved Ethan. They can't stop talking about him whenever they're with us. Their adoration makes Jack a little grumpy. I think it's totally adorable."

"They do love him and he loves them."

She wrinkled her nose again. "Then what's the problem? Isn't it a good thing to bring one more loving person into your kids' lives?"

"Well, yeah, but—"

"When you had Grace, did you love Ty any less?"

"No, but—"

"Exactly! Love is a limitless resource. Plus, isn't it a great example for your kids to see you in healthy, happy, committed relationship to a man that treats you really well? Don't you hope someday they can be happily married and have kids of their own to raise with their spouse?"

"Yes, but—"

"I know you feel bad about not being with Grace when she got hurt, but do you really think you can be within minutes of your kids all the time? Don't you travel for work? Or how about when they get older and want to go on vacation with their dad and me and our kids? You can't be an arm's length away for life. Come on, Claire, you know I'm right."

"Okay, fine! I can't always be by their side."

"So, you admit that you overreacted."

Claire puffed out a sigh. "I'll admit that the guilt of not being there for my kids may have led me to misplace blame. Doesn't matter though. Ethan and I still wouldn't have worked out."

"Why the heck not? He's so sweet and hot, and everyone can tell you make each other happy."

"Everyone?"

"Oh yeah," Gemma said, nodding her head in a big exaggerated movement. "You two were always smiling at each other or looking like you wanted to rip the other one's clothes off. It was really sweet. And hot." Her eyes brightened. "Like Ethan."

"Ethan is sweet and hot"—and a whole lot more Claire thought with another sigh—"and I love him. He's not the reason it won't work. I am."

"Why would you say that? You're great!"

Claire gave a humorless chuckle. "Gemma, you really are the nicest new wife of an ex-husband that's ever lived. While I really appreciate that you think I'm great, I know Jack doesn't agree when it comes to being in a relationship."

"OMG!" Gemma looked at her with an expression of mixed astonishment and pity. "Please do not tell me that you listened to anything Jack said about relationships. I love Jack with my whole heart, but the man is a complete idiot when it comes to how relationships work. He once said the reason we were good together was because I need him to take care of me."

"That's ridiculous! You don't need him to take care of you. You have a college degree and a good job." Claire felt her nostrils flare. "Didn't that tick you off?"

"Not at all. I understand what he means even if he doesn't completely get it. I like that Jack fills my tank with gas, does all the outside work, carries anything heavy in from the car, fixes stuff around the house, and rubs my back when my baby bump makes my muscles ache. Sure, I could do all that stuff myself, but he needs to feel needed, and I like to feel taken care of." She shrugged. "It works for us. But you're different. You don't want a man to take care of you. That's why you and Jack were so wrong for each other. You should be with a man who loves your strength and who, instead of needing to take care of you, just wants to care for you. Like Ethan."

Claire's nose started to burn as her eyes filled with tears. It was true. Ethan had told her he loved her strength and her independence. He'd never faulted her for either of those traits. Instead, he'd repeatedly tried to show her how much he cared through sweet, romantic gestures that filled her heart with happiness and her soul with love.

Gemma was right. She didn't need Ethan to take care of her. She just needed him to care for her, to love her. Forever.

"Oh, God. I made a huge mistake," she whispered, her chest constricting with panic.

Gemma took her hands and smiled knowingly. "That's okay, sweetie. We can still fix this."

Claire glanced at her watch. Ethan would be on the auction block any minute, and he was leaving town in the morning.

"How? The auction is about to start."

Squeezing each of Claire's hands at heart level between them, Gemma looked into her eyes with an intensity usually reserved for the final seconds in a World Cup match. "You're going to grab your credit card, and I'm going to drive like the wind."

SEVENTEEN

LESS than ten minutes later, Gemma angle parked in a not-so-legal spot near Fresh, and both women jumped from the car and dashed toward the crowd in the center of the Square.

When Claire reached the back of the group gathered there, she went up on tiptoes to get a view of the stage. *Holy smokes.* Microphone in hand, Kat stood center stage with Ethan beside her. She had to hurry!

"Wait! Wait! I need to say something!" She dove into the crowd. In a moment of blind panic and adrenaline-induced aggression, Claire began elbowing her way through the mass of auction attendees standing between her and the man she loved. "Excuse me. Coming through. Excuse me." Fighting her way toward the stage, she weaved around the high school principal and then the bulky backside of the town's veterinarian.

Finally reaching a clearing, she raced the last few feet and ran up the steps to the stage, leaving wide-eyed attendees and gasps of surprise in her wake. Claire grabbed the microphone from Kat's hand. "I need to say something," she whispered to her sister.

Claire shifted her gaze between Kat's triumphant

smirk and Ethan's surprised expression. She felt dizzy, her breathing rapid-fire and her heart racing. She needed to get a grip before she either face-planted or puked.

Kat shrugged a shoulder and extended her arm toward the crowd with a be-my-guest expression.

Claire death-gripped the mic and looked back at Ethan. "Hey," she mouthed, attempting a small, cautious smile.

While he didn't return any sort of smile, his expression softened and a spark of emotion flashed through his bright-blue eyes. Hoping like crazy the emotion was forgiveness and undying love, she turned to face the jam-packed square.

She cleared her throat and licked her dry lips. Holy smokes, there were a lot of people staring at her. Nearly the entire town had shown up to support Kat's fundraiser. She spotted childhood teachers, local business leaders, parents from Ty's soccer team, old friends from high school, colleagues from Bennett Industries, and many more familiar faces.

Her parents were standing off to one side with three couples Claire had known her whole life. Hannah stood nearby looking at her like she'd lost her mind—which, hell, maybe she had. Hannah's date for the night, an effervescent looking Mrs. D stood, hands clasped, beside Hannah in a blinding shade of pink.

"I'm sorry I know this isn't how auctions work, but I couldn't stand the thought of Ethan with anyone else." Claire handed her credit card to Kat. "Charge me any amount you want to buy the date with Ethan tonight. It doesn't matter. Whatever you decide, it will still be a bargain."

Claire took a shaky breath and listened to a murmur run through the crowd. She pressed her fingertips to her belly and drew more air into her lungs, desperately trying to ignore the nausea swirling through her. "Last time I was this nervous on stage was during my fourth-grade production of *A Christmas Carol.*" She gulped. "It didn't end well."

Laughter rippled through the friends and neighbors directly in front of her. Some even took a step back to what they must've assumed a safe distance from possible puke.

"I see a few of you remember as well. Since then, I've avoided drawing public attention. Well," she said, pausing to clear her throat and wipe a sweaty palm down the side of her blue jeans, "except for right now, of course."

Everywhere she looked people stared back with keen interest as the telltale pings of countless smartphone video cameras being simultaneously activated filled the night air. Her stomach rolled. She crossed her fingers that the footage wouldn't forever document how Claire Bennett lost the man she loved at her sister's fundraiser.

"Originally, my enthusiastic sister Kat registered me to be auctioned off as one of tonight's eligible bachelorettes. The only out-clause was being in a committed relationship by the night of the event." Claire braced herself, unsure how the crowd would react to her next admission. "So I asked Ethan to pretend to be my boyfriend until the event was over."

She clutched the mic to her chest, waiting for the gasps of shock, boos, or even roars of laughter to hit her. She held every muscle rigid, ready to accept whatever form of public humiliation she deserved for trying to lie her way out of a flipping charity event.

The only thing to hit her, however, was a near deathly silence. Claire glanced down at the mic pressed tightly to her chest. It was on, right? She blew into it and heard the resulting rumble of noise come from the speakers.

"We heard you, pumpkin," Mrs. D yelled. "We were just hoping for a little more exciting news than something we'd already figured out."

Claire startled in surprise. "How?"

"We know you, pumpkin," Mrs. D said. "Since ol' Jackass left you—"

"I'm right here," Jack groused from off to one side.

"Sorry. Since ol' dumbass left you," Mrs. D corrected, her voice going up a few levels, "you've been hiding away from dating like an albino vampire hides his white butt from the sun. When you started seeing Mr. Sexy Soccer Man days after he got to town, we figured something was up."

A murmur of agreement sounded through the square.

"Okay. Fine." Claire raised a hand and dipped her head in concession. "So maybe you figured that out. I bet you didn't know that somewhere along the way the emotion I was supposed to be faking become very real." She paused, waiting for the shocked reaction she'd been expecting before.

Crickets.

Seriously? Nothing? "Tough crowd," Claire muttered, looking around at the familiar, utterly unsurprised, and slightly apologetic faces staring back at her. "I'm trying to say that I love him," she snapped. Okay, she sounded more irritated than loving, but really, what the heck did it take to surprise these people?

Mrs. D looked around waiting to see if anyone else planned to speak up. When no one did, she shrugged a bony shoulder and turned back to Claire. "We sorta figured that out too, seeing as you got engaged and unengaged a few days back."

Claire's eyebrows hit her hairline. *Gemma!* She shot the younger woman a what-the-hell look.

"Sorry," Gemma mouthed, wringing her hands and looking so damn anxious, apologetic, and adorably pregnant, Claire's anger slipped away on a tired sigh.

"I panicked." Claire shook her head at the painful memory of watching Ethan's heart break in front of her. "I ended the engagement out of fear, but I was a wrong. Love is infinite. The more we give and receive it, the happier we'll be." Her voice cracked on the last word. She swallowed at the thickness in her throat and turned to see Ethan's response.

Body tense and jaw pulsing, he stared back at her with a piercing focus she'd only seen in video clips from some of his biggest games. A chill uncurled through her. Though she didn't read hatred in his eyes, she didn't exactly see forgiveness either. Cautious intensity would be the term she'd use if she had to label his scrutiny.

She licked her lips, fighting to ignore the butterflies brawling in her belly. Time for one last push before the final whistle.

"Ethan, I'd given up on fairy-tale endings until

you came into my life and turned my world and my way of thinking upside down. You showed me what it's like to be loved for who I am, flaws and all. My life is fuller, happier, more everything with you in it. You taught me that every victory is sweeter and every loss is easier when you're part of a team. You made me realize that I don't want to go through life alone. I want to be on a team. With you." She heard the crowd suck in air, but Claire kept her teary gaze locked on Ethan. "I love you."

Her face scrunched, sending tears streaming down her cheeks. "Even though it happened between us so fast my head is still spinning, I'm not going to walk away from a dream because I'm afraid of what could go wrong. If your offer still stands, I'll marry you, Ethan. I need you by my side now and forever." She repeated his words with a hesitant, hopeful smile and clung to the mic with shaking hands, willing to give the man she loved control over her fate.

Intense emotion flashed across Ethan's face, making him look older and fiercer than she'd ever seen him. He ground his jaw and shook his head. "No."

The low, raw one-word response slashed pain through her chest and choked her throat nearly closed. She'd lost him. He'd offered her his heart, and she'd been too weak to accept that precious gift before the clock ran out.

Claire locked her jaw and squeezed her eyes shut, desperate to brace herself against the god-awful anguish ripping her apart. The microphone slipped from her numb grip and landed on the stage, the speaker screeching in response. She felt the crowd jolt and could hear a grumble of disappointment but couldn't move. The crushing certainty that she'd just lost her once-in-a-lifetime love immobilized her under its overwhelming weight.

Before she crumbled to the ground, two strong hands gripped her shoulders and held firm. "No, Claire. God, I didn't mean it like that." Ethan cursed under his breath. "I meant that I won't rush you into marrying me. I've always been focused, aggressive, and even self-centered when pursuing a goal. I'm not going to do that to you. I love you too much to pressure you into marriage."

Still holding her shoulders, he leaned down so they were eye to eye and inches apart. "I want to live every day of my life with you more than anything in the world. And someday—when your head stops spinning and your feet are firmly planted on the ground and you know every single one of my annoying habits and still love me and want to be with me—we'll get married. Until then"—he shrugged a shoulder—"I'm fine taking it slow."

"I want to marry you," Claire insisted. "I know it's fast, but I'm sure—"

"So am I," Ethan interrupted with a gentle smile, taking her hands in his and dropping to one knee.

The crowd gasped, then went so quiet Claire figured the entire place could hear her heart slamming against her ribs.

"Claire Bennett, will you go out with me—for real? Forever?"

Euphoria exploded through her, swelling her heart and spreading an uncontrollable smile across her face. "Absolutely."

In an instant, Ethan was on his feet and

wrapping her in his arms. "I love you." His husky voice broke with emotion.

Claire smiled up at him. "I love you too." She threw her arms around his neck, popped to her toes, and poured all of the love and happiness flowing through her into a huge, very public kiss.

The town exploded in thunderous applause and whoops of joy.

A rumble of laughter shook Ethan's chest. Claire grinned against his lips then pulled back a fraction to look into his loving blue eyes. "Is this how it feels to score the game-winning goal?"

"Nope." He beamed his megawatt smile down on her. "This is better," he murmured, pulling her closer and brushing his lips to hers again. "So much better."

EPILOGUE

CLAIRE slipped her hand into Ethan's, rested her head back against the cushioned headrest of the luxurious ivory leather seats, and sighed in pleasure as the pointy-nosed, long-distance private jet soared high over Latin America. The early-December weekend flight was carrying the Bennett clan to Costa Rica. They were all headed to La Vida, her brother Pax's eco-resort, for the week-long celebration leading up to Pax and Sage's wedding on Saturday night.

Claire sat next to Ethan on a small couch running along the back of the plane. At the front of the jet, her parents and Ty and Grace had swiveled four oversized chairs to face each other and were playing a lively game of euchre. Mid-plane, Logan and Kat—with eight-month-old Bennett asleep on her chest—faced each other in a cozy section of plush chairs. Kat's feet were kicked onto her husband's lap for him to massage as they carried on what looked like a very entertaining conversation. Kat shot Logan a smile and a wink, and he responded with a bark of laughter. Next to them, in a single seat turned to face the back of the jet, Hannah lifted her gaze from a brick-sized, stern-looking book and rolled her eyes as if annoyed by their lovey-dovey antics.

"Whatcha reading? A love story?" Claire teased.

Hannah snorted. "No way. I'm reading about an ex-government assassin whose family was murdered by the CIA when he tried to get out of the killing business."

"Sounds heartwarming," Claire deadpanned.

Hannah shrugged. "I'm already surrounded by an unnaturally high number of lovestruck couples. Just trying to balance things out."

Claire cocked her head. "You can't believe there's too much love in the world?"

"I didn't say that." Hannah drew in a deep breath. "I'm thrilled that you and Kat and Pax have found your happily-ever-afters. But not everyone is meant to be paired off in life, and that's okay."

"Speaking of paired off ... " Kat glanced at their parents as if checking to see if they were still busy playing cards. "I should warn you, Hannah, Mom encouraged Sage to sit a particular someone beside you at the reception."

Hannah rolled her eyes. "She better not be trying to set me up with one of Pax's old high school friends again."

"It's not one of Pax's old friends. In fact, you've never met this guy," Kat said, clearly enjoying herself. "But you do know who he is."

Hannah wrinkled her brow in confusion. "Who?"

"Carter O'Reilly." Kat's voice purred with satisfaction.

Hannah shot forward in her seat, knocking the massive novel on her lap to the floor with a muffled thud. "The bad-boy Hollywood actor?"

"I heard that Pax and Sage knew him," Claire said, keeping her voice low. "I didn't realize they liked him well enough to invite him to their wedding."

"He's a good bloke," Logan interjected.

"Mom must think so too," Kat responded, her voice low and her amusement level high. "After her successful matchmaking with Pax, me, and now Claire, she's turned her attention to Hannah."

"Wait. What?" Claire shook her head and stared at Kat. "Mom didn't play matchmaker with us." She dropped her hand to Ethan's thigh.

"Pfft, right." Kat rolled her eyes. "Who do you think made sure Ethan was Ty's coach?"

Claire straightened. "Dad called the club and requested Ethan for the team."

"And who do you think was behind the scenes making sure Dad made that call?" Kat imitated twisting someone's arm and nodded toward their mom's chair.

"No way," Claire breathed, but she realized Kat could be right. Their mom had looked agitated or maybe even a little guilty at lunch the day she'd mentioned the unexpected soccer meeting she had to attend that night. "Holy smokes. It's true, isn't it?" She looked around the group.

"Don't ask me," Ethan said. "I just coached the team they told me to coach." He shrugged. "If it is true, we're going to have to get your mom one hell of a Christmas present this year."

"Oh, it's true." Kat nodded her head in large, exaggerated movements. "She's successfully hooked up three of her four kids. Guess who's next?" She grinned at Hannah.

Hannah flopped back in her seat and tossed an arm over her eyes. "This is ridiculous," she grumbled under her breath. "Why would she try to set me up with a guy who's splashed across the tabloids with a different woman each week? Carter O'Reilly lacks any sort of sexual self-restraint. From what I've read, he'll sleep with anything sporting a pair of breasts. Does she really think I'm that desperate?"

Kat opened her mouth—

"Don't answer that," Hannah whisper-hissed. "I'm done talking about this." She snatched her book from the floor and slammed it open on her lap, staring deliberately at the pages.

"Fine. I'll drop it." Kat held up one hand in a show of surrender and patted sleeping Bennett on the back. "Just thought you'd want to know."

"I can't believe I didn't see it sooner," Claire murmured to Ethan. She leaned back and closed her eyes.

"Are you ticked your mom maneuvered us together?" Ethan whispered in her ear.

"How could I be upset with her?" She rolled her head back and forth on the soft leather, a smile tugging at her lips. "I'm more content, happy, and in love than I've ever been. Thanks to you." She opened her eyes to look at him on the last word.

His eyes lit with mischief. "I've got an idea on how to make you even more content, happy, and in love with me." He shifted his gaze to the bathroom door and then back to her, one eyebrow raised.

Unfortunately for Ethan, his twitching lips and barely suppressed laughter ruined any serious attempt at seduction.

"Shush." Claire swatted his hard thigh. "I've had to go to the bathroom for the past hour, but I knew you'd tease me if I even mentioned that room."

"Can't help it." He raised their joined hands and brushed an electrifying kiss on the inside of her wrist. "That experience changed my entire outlook on air travel."

"You're going to bring it up every time we're on a plane for the rest of our lives, aren't you?" Claire gave a resigned laugh.

He blasted her with the thousand-watt, dimpled smile she loved nearly as much as the man who wielded it. "Absolutely."

Claire leaned closer, placed her palm on his chest, and dropped her voice to a sultry whisper. "Next time we're alone, we should re-create the experience in some other"—she let a slow, suggestive smile slide across her lips—"surprising location."

He sucked in air. "Thought you didn't like surprises?"

"I like *your* surprises, Ethan."

He tipped his head back and laughed. "Call me Lucky." He pulled her tighter to his side. "After all, I am lucky in love."

Claire thought about the lifetime full of love and laughter ahead of them. She snuggled closer to Ethan and brushed a soft kiss against his cheek. "We both are."

Thank You

Thanks for reading Lucky in Love*! If you have a moment, I hope you'll consider writing a quick review. In today's world, reviews are a great way for readers to find new authors and authors to find new readers. And it's wonderful people like you who make that happen!*

Book four in my Silver Bay series features Hannah Bennett's romance and will be available in December of 2018. Please join my VIP list at www.ameliajudd.com if you'd like to receive an email on release day.

Happy reading!
Amelia

About the Author

Award-winning author Amelia Judd writes fun and flirty contemporary romance. She loves to entertain her readers with memorable characters and fast-paced plots that blend humor, heart, and heat.

After receiving a degree in international affairs, Amelia lived and studied in Belgium for over three years. During her time in Europe, she traveled extensively, earned a master's degree, and fell in love with writing contemporary romance.

Amelia now lives in the Midwest with her sports-loving husband, two active kids, and a lovable dog that stays by her side day and night. When she isn't writing, she's spending time with family, hanging out with friends, chauffeuring her kiddos around town, sneaking off to the movies, or planning her family's next getaway.

Connect with Amelia Judd online:

www.ameliajudd.com

www.facebook.com/author.amelia.judd/

amelia@ameliajudd.com

www.goodreads.com/Amelia_Judd